CITY OF THE DEAD

CULLEN & BAIN 1

ED JAMES

OTHER BOOKS BY ED JAMES

SCOTT CULLEN MYSTERIES SERIES

1. GHOST IN THE MACHINE
2. DEVIL IN THE DETAIL
3. FIRE IN THE BLOOD
4. STAB IN THE DARK
5. COPS & ROBBERS
6. LIARS & THIEVES
7. COWBOYS & INDIANS
8. HEROES & VILLAINS

CULLEN & BAIN NOVELLAS

1. CITY OF THE DEAD
2. WORLD'S END

CRAIG HUNTER SERIES

1. MISSING
2. HUNTED
3. THE BLACK ISLE

DS VICKY DODDS

1. TOOTH & CLAW

DI SIMON FENCHURCH SERIES

1. THE HOPE THAT KILLS
2. WORTH KILLING FOR
3. WHAT DOESN'T KILL YOU
4. IN FOR THE KILL
5. KILL WITH KINDNESS

6. KILL THE MESSENGER

MAX CARTER SERIES

1. TELL ME LIES

SUPERNATURE SERIES

1. BAD BLOOD
2. COLD BLOOD

PROLOGUE

RICH

I hit the button and step away from the bin lorry. The metal jaws crunch the cardboard and swallow it all down. Good work!

'Let's go!' Big Jim pulls himself up to the handhold and thumps the side of the lorry. His belly hangs out the bottom of his Celtic home shirt, the green-and-white hoops smeared with all sorts of muck.

An audiobook blares out of the speakers in the cabin, some ridiculous post-apocalyptic crap about Nazis and zombies, or something, but Billy the driver seems to hear the signal, as the lorry rumbles off down the street.

Big Jim hangs there, scratching his nose with his gloved wrist. 'Keep up, you big South African bastard!'

'Nothing wrong with South Africa, mate.' I grab the handle and haul myself up with the kind of grace Big Jim can only ever dream of. I'm topless, just like every other day, and my abs look awesome in this light. The definition is perfect. 'Like to see you in Jo'burg. Wouldn't survive five fucking minutes.'

'Ah grew up here in Glasgow, pal. Handle that, can handle anything.'

'You didn't grow up, mate.' I hang on as the lorry trundles along the dark street. In the distance, the sun pops up over the horizon, giving a flash of light against the tower blocks in the distance and the old tower in the graveyard just over the road behind the factories. 'Beautiful sky, eh?'

'No' as beautiful as *that*, I tell you.' Big Jim waves at the pavement.

Two schoolgirls trudge along in the darkness, passing between cones of light, tapping at their phones, oblivious to the middle-aged pervert ogling them. Short skirts, black tights, school ties barely done up over their low blouses. Maybe fourteen. *Maybe.*

Sick, sick bastard.

I shoot Jim a scowl, raising my eyebrows to show how harshly I'm judging the seedy creep. 'Mate, they're really young.'

'Aye, well.' Big Jim gives me a leery grin, his tongue hanging loose. 'Grass on the pitch, eh?'

'Sick bastard.'

It's my turn to slap the side of the lorry and I hop off before Billy pulls it to a stop. I gave him the thumbs up, not that Billy tears himself away from his gripping audiobook. I kind of want to tell him about Big Jim, but he's never interested in all that banter.

Fuck him.

I sidle off up the lane, but my trousers slip lower with each step. Christ, I need some new strides.

Next up—just like every bloody week—are three bins that the hipster bastards in the microbrewery haven't wheeled out to the road. They're sitting in the factory car park, one flickering light catching them.

Usually a two-man job to shift each one, but I always like to try to move them on my own.

Could leave them, but we got a fuckton of hassle from the boss last time we didn't take them out. Some bastard in the factories must've phoned in to complain.

Big Jim raises a gloved hand in front of my face. 'Dinnae mention that to the boys at the depot, right?'

'What, that you're a fucking paedo?'

'I'm no' a *paedo*.' Jim's scowling at me, but I can't tell if it's one of anger or confusion. 'Those were lassies, no' boys!'

Confusion, then.

'Mate, it's not about their gender, it's about their *age*.'

Big Jim seems flummoxed by that. 'Nothing wrong with admiring the female form.' His chin dimples as he snarls. 'You're the one who's a poof. Now *that's* unnatural.'

'I'm not having this chat again.' I set off up the lane towards the dumpsters. 'I'll do these myself.'

Big Jim doesn't disagree. He tears off a glove and leans back against the lorry, phone out already. Hate to think what that sick bastard is watching on that thing, or who he's contacting and about what.

Maybe the prick's getting ahead of me, calling up the boss and pre-emptively defending against any shit coming his way.

I'll get the fucker if he does.

I stop and grab the first dumpster's handle, flexing my biceps and pectorals.

And there she is. Same as every week, the woman in the flat above is looking down. Damp hair scraped back in a towel, her dressing gown open wide enough to show her cleavage.

I give her a saucy wink, even though she's about eight inches short of being my type. Nice to be admired, eh? Then she's gone, her curtains shut.

And this bastard dumpster isn't fucking moving. I grab the handle again, but another sharp tug and it still doesn't budge. The front wheels look knackered.

Big Jim's marching up the lane. He grabs my arm. 'Rich, that was—'

'Get the fuck off me, man!' I swivel round and get into the basic stance, ready to fight, ready to win. 'Those gloves are fucking disgusting!'

'Chill oot, you radge bastard.' Big Jim holds his mobile in an ungloved hand. His Celtic shirt is covered over by an acid-yellow high-viz jacket. 'Davie says to make sure you've got your top on.'

'I keep telling him, I don't wear a top. This temperature is fucking perfect for fat burning.'

'Anyone ever tell you that you're a weird bastard?' Big Jim reaches for the handle. 'Here, let us help.'

Course I know what Big Jim's up to here. Trying to get in my good favours so I don't mention the under-age perving to the other lads. 'I've got this.'

'Doesn't look that way to me. This is a two-man bin, and if there's one thing I know it's—' Big Jim screws up his face, nostrils twitching. 'What's that smell?'

'Can't smell anything.'

'It's *minging*.' Big Jim grabs the lever and pulls it, popping the lid. 'Have a deek inside, bud. I'll hold it for you.'

'If it'll shut you up.' I vault up and hold myself there, peering into the bin.

The rubbish is piled up along the side, stacked-up cardboard boxes and loose wrapping plastic. Some arsehole has piled in a sodden rug stained by God knows what that must weigh half a ton by itself. I'm looking at what's beyond it, though, when the bin judders as Jim hauls himself up for a peek. He gasps when he sees it too.

A man lies in a puddle of bleach, naked except for a nappy. Eyes wide open and very, very dead.

1

CULLEN

Acting Detective Inspector Scott Cullen's brain hurt. Not even nine and he was close to wanting to chuck it all in and head home for the day. It was that or get something to eat. He was *starving*.

Detective Chief Inspector Colin Methven crouched at the end of the table. His cheap black suit hung off his runner's frame, his wild eyebrows searching the air like TV antennas. He stood up tall and tossed another sheet of paper to Cullen, as if he could cope with the ten or so he already had. 'I need you to make some decisions here, Scott. It's called being a manager. This needs to be with Carolyn Soutar's office by close of play today. Okay?'

'Fine.' Cullen looked at the latest one. Yet another page of data for the team size review, showing a structure of one DS to his six DCs. Something wasn't right on it. Just... What? He scanned it again. 'Why isn't Bain on here?'

Methven took the seat next to Cullen. 'I'm presenting you with another option. You know I need to cut costs across the department. Losing a sergeant, especially *him*, would aid that matter greatly.'

'You're asking me to do that role as well as this, aren't you?'

'Scott, you're an Acting DI. If you want to permanently step up, I need you to make the hard decisions. Do you really need DS Bain?'

'No, but if it's a choice between him and nobody, I'll take him.'

'Well, I could bring in Lauren Reid from Al Buchan's team. She was a DS down in Berkshire, I think. And I know an excellent DS in Dundee who could do a job.' Methven checked his phone. 'Oh, sodding hell.' He put it to his ear and left the room in a rush. 'Carolyn, hi. We're just looking at it now.'

Cullen folded the page in half and stood up. Time for breakfast.

CULLEN CARRIED his tray through the station canteen. As he walked, his coffee bubbled through the sip hole, covering the rest of the lid in a thin black film, but luckily it kept away from his egg roll.

His team had pulled two window tables together, and were laughing and joking. Five DCs and a DS in tell-tale suits like they were working in a normal office. Outside, two buses wrestled their way past each other, one heading to central Edinburgh, the other way out into the southside sticks.

Cullen couldn't face spending any more time with his team. Time was, he'd seen inspectors sitting only with their own grades and thought it was pathetic. Now he was there, well. He dumped his tray on a free table in the corner. He shrugged his suit jacket onto the chair back and slouched into his seat, then eased the lid off his coffee, but still managed to spill it everywhere.

The wall of white noise around him was like a soothing blanket, a safe place to hide. Mainly from managing a team making a mess of case preparation, and from his boss. But it was also time away from his desk, maybe time to play a game on his phone. He checked through the messages—nothing looked pressing—and let himself enjoy a long yawn before squirting brown sauce onto his fried egg roll. He shut the lid and let it all congeal, then settled back and started flinging cartoon birds at evil pigs.

'Morning, Sundance.' DS Brian Bain dumped his tray and sat opposite. The plate was overstuffed with a fry up. Streaky bacon, haggis circle, tatty scone, fried bread, hash browns and a sea of beans walled off by three pink sausages that seemed barely cooked. The kind of mess Cullen's mum would call a cooked breakfast, the euphemism that made a coronary-inducing meal sound almost pleasant.

As tired as the breakfast looked, Bain looked worse. The dirty grey stubble on his head matched the pale skin and the fuzzy goatee he'd been sporting for the last few months. And he had a massive red boil on his nose. 'I fuckin' swear it's impossible to get a decent breakfast in this shite town.'

Cullen felt his shoulders sag, wishing the inevitable heart attack would strike Bain down sooner rather than later. 'You missed this morning's briefing.'

'Sorry, *boss*.' Bain snarled the words. Time was, Cullen had to work for the prick, but Bain hadn't got used to them flipping roles. He bit the end off a sausage and started eating, his lips slapping together. 'Only place you can get a good fry up's in Glasgow, Sundance. God's own fuckin' city.'

'You're welcome to put in for a transfer.'

'They wouldn't take me. Your fault I ended up back here, anyway. Those pips on your shoulder were mine to start with.'

Cullen looked at his shoulder, but all he saw was navy suit jacket. 'You can't blame me for taking them when you dropped a bollock on it, can you? And you never tire of banging on about it.'

'Natural order of things has been disrupted, Sundance.' Bain scooped a mound of beans into his mouth and chewed, mouth open. 'Absolute shambles, this place.'

Cullen took another glug of coffee. He could start defending himself and the city he'd made his home a good few years back, but what would be the point? Bain would be on to something else. 'So go elsewhere, then.'

But Bain just sat there, chewing away, no doubt happy to be sitting with an inspector rather than the rank and file, even if the inspector in question was Cullen.

'There you are.' Methven stood there, fizzing with energy— or coffee—like he couldn't handle being at rest.

'Sorry, sir, I just got hungry. I'll get back to it—'

'That can wait. Someone found a body in the East End this morning, looks like murder.'

Cullen frowned. 'East End? Don't you mean Leith?'

'I mean Glasgow.'

Bain's eyebrows flashed up. 'Oh, aye?'

'Caledonia Street.'

'That's no' the fuckin' East End, Col. That's the Gorbals!'

'Well, either way, both of their MITs are occupied, so they've passed the case to us.' Methven had the look of someone desperate to score points against his rivals. 'Can you go through and get a head start? I'll follow once I've finished my morning meetings.'

'Nae luck, Sundance.'

Cullen took another look at his team over at the other table, but instead stood up, swiping a hash brown off Bain's plate. 'You're coming with me. Be just like old times, eh?'

2

Cullen walked along the street *again*, checking his phone *again*. Somehow he'd lost Bain on the motorway through from Edinburgh. He hit dial once more, but it just went to voicemail.

A hulking gorilla of a detective in a cheap suit blocked off access to the crime scene, his orange tan clearly from a bottle. The yellow tape flickered in the breeze behind him. A dark brick lane led up to the backs of a row of factories deep in banjo country. Some forensics officers worked away in a bin pressed against the side wall, a pair of bright lights blaring out into the dull Glasgow morning. Officers in pristine white crime scene suits were rummaging around inside another bin.

A bin lorry was parked down the side street, with three workers sitting in the cabin. Didn't look like anyone was talking. Finding a dead body would do that to you.

Cullen wanted to have a word, but he really should wait for Bain. As soon as he could, he needed the creepy little bastard to split off and run some angle of the investigation that meant they didn't spend any time together. Counting paperclips, something like that. Any task where he couldn't make an arse of anything important. How he managed to survive in Police Scotland was a constant mystery.

Behind, the factories advertised their wares. A car wash, a

lighting showroom, hot-tub hire and a hipster brewery with a tap room. Who in their right mind would come out here for a pint?

Some new houses lurked off to the side, affordable housing they'd call them. Maybe social housing. He'd passed some less social stuff on the way in, Sixties boxes that'd started in hell and just descended. Judgment aside, there might be some witnesses over the way.

And further behind, in front of the dual multi-storey towers was the Southern Necropolis. The City of the Dead. Ancient graves that now looked like a croquet lawn led up to a circular tower, really old like some mausoleum, and completely incongruous with the surrounding houses. Seeing it gave Cullen pause, made him think of all the recent deaths in his life. Time was, everything felt like it'd last forever, but now... Now he was getting older and things seemed to change every five minutes. He could remember afternoons lasting months, but now months passed like an hour.

In a roar of Dire Straits, a purple Mondeo cut the corner and parked way too close to Cullen's car. *Money for Nothing* was mercifully cut short and Bain got out, sucking in a deep breath like he'd climbed one of the Cairngorms. 'Ah, you don't get air like this in Edinburgh, Sundance.' He took in the breeze like it was perfume.

All Cullen could smell was dirty diesel, cigarette smoke and stale piss. Still, it hadn't rained. Yet. Always in the post through here, though.

Cullen was beginning to regret choosing to work with Bain again. Only upside was he knew Glasgow. Brought up here, plus two stints in CID. 'Come on.' He led the way over to the crime scene.

The gorilla stopped them with a deep grunt. Cullen hoped he had the opposable thumbs to work the pen and the clipboard. 'Sign here.'

One of the suited figures working the bins clocked them and jogged over, clawing at his mask. DC Damian McCrea, an old colleague of Bain's, gasping for breath. Bald head and a good three stone over regulation weight. 'Alright, gaffer!'

Cullen groaned again. This case couldn't get any worse now, and he'd not even seen the body.

'Damo, good to see you.' Bain grabbed him in a big hug and started singing *The Boys Are Back In Town* but got lost halfway through the chorus.

McCrea broke free and did a double take. 'Cullen?' He gave Bain a snide grin. 'Christ, gaffer, you brought the village idiot with you?'

'And I thought you were more than enough idiot for a whole city.' Cullen gave him a wide grin, trying to hide his burning rage. 'Brian works for me. I'm a DI now.'

'*Acting* DI.'

Cullen let Bain have it, kept his glare on McCrea. 'Are you bin raking, Damian?'

'For my sins. Not found anything, mind.' With a shrug, McCrea thumbed behind him. 'You want to see the body?'

Bain started off. 'Hold me back.'

The gorilla with the clipboard grabbed him by the jacket. 'Get a suit on, you clown.'

~

'I WANT to call it a dumpster, Sundance, but it's . . . just a big fuckin' bin.' Bain wrestled a set of ladders into position and started clambering up. 'Right?' At the top, he peered inside. 'In the name of the fuckin' wee man.' He started back down the ladder again. 'Christ alive. I've seen some pretty fucked-up things in my time, but...' His grey pallor had turned pure white. 'Here, Sundance, you take a look.'

Cullen waited for him to shimmy down then shot up the ladder. Near the top, he got a blast of a bleach stink mixed with human shit. He almost lost his egg roll. Breathing through his mouth, he took the last couple of rungs a lot slower, his gut gurgling away, then stopped at the top, mindful of whatever the hell was inside had just done to Bain, a seasoned detective. He looked inside the bin.

ICI male. Mid-forties, maybe. Thick hair covered his torso, right up his back. A puddle of clear liquid ran halfway up his chest. That'd be the bleach then. He lay face up, eyes open, staring right at Cullen. Naked except for an adult-sized nappy, white but soiled.

McCrea clambered up another ladder and started huffing yet another ladder over into the bin.

Cullen focused on him instead of the corpse. 'Surprised to see you here, Damian. Thought your mob were too busy to take this case.'

'Aye, my DCI caught a shooting down Pollockshaws way the other morning.' McCrea finished resting the second ladder inside and grinned. 'Can see you know the place, but can't mind which one's the posh bit? Way I remember the difference is, Pollockshiels shields you from Pollockshaws.'

'I wasn't, but thanks. Doesn't explain why I've got you, though.'

'This has all the hallmarks of a serial rape case I've been working.'

That prickled Cullen's neck. 'All the hallmarks, eh?'

'You know what I mean. People waking up in bins, wearing adult nappies, but with no idea how they got there. And with very sore arseholes and fannies.' Talking about rape victims like that didn't seem to faze McCrea. 'Anyway, this could be a copycat, could be unconnected, could be anything. The gaffer's got me on it to stop you eastie beasties making an arse of it.'

'If anyone's an expert in making an arse of—'

'Ha, ha, ha.'

Cullen looked around the lane. Only one camera he could see. 'You got any CCTV?'

'Two cameras in vicinity. Both gubbed.'

'How?'

'Austerity. They break down and they don't get fixed.'

'Get down from there, you hooligan!' Sounded like a woman, the nasal rasp of a local. A very, very angry one. Cullen looked round. A masked figure was shaking her fists at him.

Cullen took his time getting down.

McCrea was back rooting around in the other bin, not taking much care as he tossed evidence bags on the brick paving. Astonishing how quickly a fat man can move when an authority figure appears.

At the bottom, the interloper was shouting the odds at Bain, her words muffled by her mask.

'Tell me about it.' Bain nodded. 'Absolutely shocking who they let into crime scenes these days.'

She was scowling at Cullen. 'Who the hell are you?'

'DI Scott Cullen.' He got out his warrant card. 'This is DS Bain. DCI Methven sent us through from Edinburgh.'

'Ah, well. Come with me.' The woman led them off to a safe distance, then tore off her crime scene mask. Ruby red lipstick and pale white skin, with a curl of ginger hair poking out of her hood. 'Rachel Gibson. I'm one of the pathologists.' She led them back towards the perimeter and the gorilla with his clipboard. 'How much do you know?'

'Assume fuck all.' Bain let his own mask dangle free. 'Give us the whole shooting match, darlin'.'

'Do you mind not calling me that?'

'Sorry. I'm a local lad, but been based through in Edinburgh for way too long. Some of their caveman ways must've rubbed off on me.'

'Right.' Gibson started unzipping her crime scene suit. 'Well, I've finished my initial assessment. I was checking up on the whereabouts of the transport. I need to get our victim on the slab to complete the job.'

Cullen got between her and Bain, aware that he was pulling some alpha male bullshit, but it was the only language Bain understood. 'You say victim. He was definitely murdered?'

'I've not been up close and personal with him in my lab yet, but my initial assessment would be that he's been asphyxiated by strangulation.' She dragged a pale finger across her own throat. 'Several bruises there. And I know you'll want time of death, but all I can say is the poor fellow died last night. Livor mortis would suggest that he's been in situ for roughly ten hours.'

Cullen tried to follow through a strand of logic. And he couldn't.

Why the hell would a grown man wear a nappy? Aside from

incontinence, he had a million reasons buzzing around his head, most of them pointing to some form of sexual deviance. The links to McCrea's cases, though. He needed to confirm that connection or shut it down.

He stared back at the bin. 'What's with the nappy?'

'I had a... little prod and the nappy's been heavily soiled, meaning the nappy was most likely on when he died. I'd suggest that either your killer's a pervert—'

A big laugh from Bain interrupted her.

Her glare suggested it wasn't the reaction she was looking for. 'Or your killer wanted to utilise forensic countermeasures such as immersion in bleach, but morally they couldn't stand the indignity of a naked body. Either way, gentlemen, that liquid he's in is bleach. You're not getting any biologicals off the body.'

Cullen nodded slowly. The logic was thinning out even more. Definitely someone covering their tracks.

'If the cause of death turns out to be manual strangulation, you could measure the span of the hand and rule suspects in or out accordingly.'

'If? What are the odds it's something else, not murder?'

'It could very well be death by misadventure. I need to conduct a full post mortem before we find out, but I'd say it looks like murder, yes, and strangulation.'

Either way, treating it like a murder was preferable to not.

Bain shrugged. 'I mean, if you truss your victims up in nappies, it'll stop the jobbies and that coming out when he dies. Makes them easier to dispose of and remove the traces.'

Gibson winced. 'While your colleague's a tad crass, yes, it'd prevent a mess at death. The anal sphincter releases tension and excretes in a lot of cases. But like I say, I need to get him on the slab and confirm my findings.'

It was starting to turn into something, anyway. 'You got any idea who found him?'

~

'So I found that bloke, eh?' Rich Petersen was leaning

against a wall, his sharp South African accent slicing through the city drone. Top off, showing off his ripped torso and a giant tattoo of a Chinese dragon crawling round his neck. He shot a glare at Bain. 'Hey, mate, you mind not checking me out, eh?'

'You fancy putting on a top?'

'Never wear one.' Petersen folded his arms, seemed to flex his biceps. 'Even in winter. Never gets *that* cold here.'

Cullen turned the page in his notebook. 'So you were on a round this morning, right?'

'Commercial bins today, mate. All the fucking shop waste, eh? Absolute fucking nightmare.'

'These big bins...' Bain sniffed. 'Any idea what they call them?'

'Dumpsters.'

'Thought so.' Bain flicked up an eyebrow at Cullen.

The pathology van peeped its horn and they got out of the way. Their unidentified body was heading elsewhere.

Cullen leaned in to whisper: 'You're cramping my style here. Can you take the other scaffie?'

'The other *what*?'

'The other binman.'

'What the fuck is a scaffie?'

'My gran used to call binmen scaffies.'

'Teuchter bastard.' Bain shook his head, then smiled at the bigger, older binman. He'd barely said a word. 'Right, sir, let's give these two some peace.' He led over towards his car.

Cullen smiled at Rich Petersen. 'Sorry about that.'

'Happens all the time, mate. But God sculpted me, eh?'

Cullen pretended to scratch his chin to stop himself laughing. 'So you were checking those dumpsters?'

'Damn right, I was.' Petersen nodded over at the crime scene. 'Usually, some fucker's flytipped a tin of paint in one. Happens all the fucking time, mate, and makes a fucking massive mess.' His expression darkened and he seemed to shiver. 'But I found the fella in there this morning. Fucking weirdest thing I ever saw, mate, and I saw some shit back in Jo'burg.'

Cullen didn't want to know, so he left him some space.

Petersen patted Cullen's shoulder. 'You mind if I leave, mate? These bins won't clear themselves, eh?'

'Just got a couple more questions, sir.' Cullen gave him a cold smile and passed him the forensics tablet, showing a high-resolution image of the dead-eyed face from below. 'You recognise this man?'

Petersen gave it a good look. 'Nah, mate. Sorry. Never seen this guy in my life until...' He broke off, jaw clenched.

As far as Cullen could tell, Petersen had nothing to do with this, save finding a corpse. In a bin. Covered in bleach. Wearing a nappy. 'Need to know your movements last night.'

'Seriously?'

'Afraid so.'

Petersen sighed. 'Okay, so I was out on the piss with a mate, then back home for some sleep. Early start, eh?'

'He got a name, this mate?'

'She. Her name's Marie. Marie Gray.'

Cullen clicked his pen. 'Can you give me her number?'

'This is a fucking joke.' But Petersen complied.

Cullen finished taking it down, then pocketed his notebook and gave him a business card. 'Give me a call if anything jogs your memory, okay?'

'Sure thing, mate.' Petersen wandered off towards the bin lorry. He stopped to hoik up his trousers, muttering, 'Need some new strides...'

3

Bain

Tell you, that Sundance is a fuckin' cheeky bastard. Thinking he's the boss of me. Used to be an arrogant prick of a DC, supposed to take orders from yours fuckin' truly way back when, but now he's an acting DI he's even more fuckin' annoying. And useless.

The binman gives us a frown. Big Jim. Hair coming out of his lugs. Keeps squinting too. Dirty big bastard, though, nose as red as the Aberdeen home top and just as fuckin' dirty. And he's wearing an old Celtic shirt, least it looks that way under all the muck it's covered in. Enough said about him. Actually, he fuckin' stinks. And not just 'cos he's a binman, or a fuckin' scaffie as Sundance calls it, but the ripest BO. Can see the type a mile off: soon as he clocks off he's in the boozer sucking down eighteen pints, then stumbles back home and straight to bed, then gets up without even a Bathgate shower, and I mean washing his oxters in the sink. 'You even listening to me, pal?'

Takes a second to realise he's talking to me. 'Sure, I'm listening.'

Big Jim frowns at us. He's a right shifty one, that's for sure.

No wedding rings under those great big binmen gloves, meaning he's not that experienced at lying, if you catch my drift. Maybe there's an ex-Mrs Big Jim, maybe Mad Ange or something, who he's lied to. Got to keep an open mind about these things. 'Well, like I was saying, I was at a mate's last night.'

'Aye? Any way you can prove that?'

'Struggling to think of how, eh?' Big Jim's lost to me for a few secs, staring across the road. A young lassie walks past, pushing a pram, phone to her ear. Tight leggings. One of those where you wonder if that's her kid or her younger brother or sister. Looks really fuckin' young is what I'm trying to say here.

Either way, Big Jim is a dirty, dirty bastard.

I wave my hand in front of his face. 'I said, what were you doing?'

'Oh, aye. Yeah. Eh, watching some films.'

Probably the kind of pornos that'd make your eyes water, if this boy's wandering eye that satisfies his soul has anything to do with it. 'Anything good?'

He's back staring at us. 'A Van Damme and a Segal.'

'Old ones?'

'Nah, new ones. Well, new-ish. Utter shite too.'

'Rightio.' Take a few seconds to note it all down, but nothing else comes to mind. 'Must've been pretty freaky finding that body?'

He nods. 'Not my first rodeo, bud.'

'Aye?'

'Hear about these rapes? Few of them over the last six months or so. Well, yours truly found one of the lassies in a bin up in Partick. Out of her skelp on Christ knows what. It's a bloody plague, I tell you.'

And you just put yourself in the fuckin' frame, pal. He gets a wave of my notebook. 'I'll give you bell later, aye? Keep your phone on.'

'Sure thing.' He holds it up. Expensive-looking Samsung monster. And there's this cute wee lassie's face on the screen. Boy's a pervert, that's for sure. He lumbers off. Big Jim. Boy lifts weights, but he also lifts pints to his lips and stuffs as many carbs as he can fit in that fat pus of his.

Takes patting a few pockets until I find my blower, but there it is. Trouser, front left. Should've started there. Speed dial number three. 'Elvis, bud, you busy?'

Cheeky sod sighs down the line. 'Suspect I'm about to be.'

'Need you to check the location of this boy's phone last night.'

A deeper sigh. Worse than fuckin' Sundance. That, or sighing is like that new plague from fuckin' China or something. Coronavirus or whatever it's called. Stick a fuckin' lime in your neck! 'I'll see what I can find, Brian.'

'Good man. We still on for Sunday?'

'Aye, just got a delivery of IPAs from Canada. Some interesting stuff in it. Flying Monkeys, Nickelbrook and a new Collective Arts Double IPA. Mind how much you liked the last one?'

'Looking forward to sampling this one, then. Cheers.' The phone goes back in the trousers, so maybe next time I won't have to hunt for it.

That other binman, the South African boy, hops up on the back and thumps the side. The lorry trundles off in a belch of dirty diesel. Top off like it's the fuckin' weather for it.

'Tell you, Sundance, I've seen everything. A fuckin' sexy binman.'

The snide bastard frowns at me. 'Sexy?'

'In my day, they were all big fat hoofers with drink problems. He's a total deviant.'

A dark grey Range Rover pulls up next to us, the engine still running as the window rolls down. Fuckin' Methven pokes his skinny bastard face out at us. Walrus eyebrows. 'You getting anywhere?'

He gets a shake of the head. 'Aye, give us a minute, Col, eh?'

'I was talking to Scott.'

Before I go tonto, Sundance chips in. 'Thought you weren't coming through for a while, sir?'

'Called in a few favours. Rachel's going to run the PM now.'

Fuck it, I give him a flash of the old eyebrows. 'Rachel, aye?' Let him know I'm onto him.

'Settle down, Brian.' Prick glares at us. 'Dr Gibson used to be based in Aberdeen when I was in Grampian police.' His window starts rolling up. 'If you need me, call me.' And he fucks off down the street without even a glance at the lane.

'Prick could've called.' Give him a flick of the Vs.

Sundance laughs at us. Looks grudging, but fuck it. Beggars can't be choosers. Bet he's wishing Methven clocked me giving him the Vs. 'Not many things I agree with you about.'

I wave over at the bin lorry. 'What's your take on this, Sundance?'

'Until we get an ID, we're snookered.' He's buggering about with the forensics tablet. 'That's just a dead guy in a bin. Forties, white, but that's about it.'

'Tell me about it, Sundance. Tell me about it.'

'Hoy!' Damo McCrea's charging towards us, grinning away like a dog with two cocks who's just found a third. 'What did you think of the body? Pretty sick, right?'

Actually gives us a flash of the poor bastard in the bin. Almost makes us boak. 'Something like that, aye. You cleared off sharpish when the doctor pitched up.'

'Aye, well. She doesn't like us.'

'What did you do?'

'Nothing. She's a snob. End of.'

Sundance butts in, trying to act the wide bastard here. 'You got any idea who the victim is?'

'Aye.'

'Care to share with us?'

Damo waves an evidence bag in Sundance's face. 'Found this in the other bin along with four empty bleach bottles.'

Sundance snatches it off him. A wallet. Prick rummages round, opening the thing, then shoves it in my face. Takes a good squint for us to focus, but it's a driver's license, belonging to one Paul Skinner. Give or take a few bottles of bleach, the ID photo's a good match for the face on Sundance's forensics tablet. That's the boy in the bin, near as damn it.

Damo's shifting his gaze between us like an overkeen puppy. 'So, we're hotfooting round there, aye?'

'Nope.' Sundance fuckin' grins at the boy. '*We* are, but you're going to get your forensics guys to run the prints on this wallet.'

'Ah, fuck sake.'

'Just do it, okay?' Even hands over a business card with something scribbled on the back. 'Then I need you to check this alibi for me. This Marie Gray, who he was supposed to be with the guy who found the body. Bain's sexy binman.'

'Sundance, I fuckin' swear—'

4

CULLEN

Paul Skinner lived in a Victorian villa on the Southside. A storey and a half of beige stone, with a cream bay window poking out from behind a row of pot plants in the small front garden, filled with pebbles and grasses still thriving in the cold.

'Nice pad, Sundance.' Bain strolled up the front path, whistling, hands in pockets like he wasn't visiting a murder victim's home. 'You want to have a wee practice at giving a death message?'

'You're assuming he wasn't single.'

Bain stopped outside the door. 'So you missed his wedding ring?'

Cullen felt himself blush. Never good when Bain had got more out of a crime scene than him.

'His wife'll need some comforting, Sundance. You up to it?'

They had one of those fancy video doorbells. Ring, judging by the logo. Cullen pressed it and it lit up, letting out rising chimes.

'You ignoring me?'

'Let's just get this over with, aye?'

'Think we should get a few more bodies through here. Half your team's pissing about on Schoolbook all day.'

'Which ones?'

'Not today, sorry.' A disembodied voice burst out of a speaker, thin and shrill.

'Police, sir. DS Bain.' He thrust out his warrant card. 'This is DI Cullen.'

The door opened. A thin man in his forties peered out through thick glasses. 'What's up?'

'Looking to speak to someone about a Paul Skinner.'

The man seemed to deflate. 'What's he done?'

'You got a name, sir?'

'My name's Gavin. Gavin Whitecross.' Red eyes flicked between them. 'What's going on?'

'His wife in?'

'Wife? Paul's my husband.'

A frown flickered across Bain's forehead. 'Have you seen him today?'

Whitecross clasped his hands together and dipped his head, like he was praying. 'Not since yesterday. He... didn't come home last night.'

'That a common occurrence?'

Whitecross scowled at Bain. 'You need to tell me *right now* what he's done.'

Cullen stepped between them. 'Mr Whitecross, I'm afraid we found your husband's body this morning.'

~

ONE THING GLASGOW had going for it was a much better-specced mortuary than Edinburgh. Cullen thought it was probably due to the higher frequency of murders in the city, but he wouldn't say that out loud, at least not while he was still in it.

Through a glass wall crisscrossed with thin mesh, Dr Gibson lifted up a sheet and showed Paul Skinner's pale face.

Standing next to her, Gavin Whitecross took one look, then nodded at Dr Gibson. 'That's him.' His voice was distorted through the speakers, though Cullen couldn't see any. White-cross shut his eyes. Tears streaked down his cheeks and he had to grip the edge of a table.

Dr Gibson opened the door and let Whitecross back out into their custody. She didn't seem the sort to want to spend too much time with members of the public, at least not when they were still breathing.

Whitecross stumbled towards Cullen, looking like he might collapse any second. And he did, but Cullen caught him. 'Hey, let's get you a cup of tea.' His turn to nod at Dr Gibson, then he led Whitecross through the doorway into the family room, all subtle shades of beige.

Bain was already in there, pouring tea into a small cup. 'How do you take it?'

Whitecross collapsed into a seat and slumped back. 'Usually drink coffee. But milk, please.'

Bain poured milk in, then gave a reptilian grin as he spooned in some sugar. 'Here you are.' He slid the cup across the table and started pouring another two cups.

'Thanks.' Whitecross sipped some tea, wincing slightly. 'This is really hard for me.'

Bain was scowling. 'Just—'

'It's okay, sir.' Cullen blew on his tea. He wanted to give Whitecross a few minutes, see if it shook anything loose. He smiled, warm and full of understanding, or at least he hoped so. 'Take your time.'

And Whitecross did, just sitting there, staring into space. Sometimes when you broke the news to someone, they broke in half there and then. Sometimes it never happened. But sometimes seeing their spouse's body on a slab, that was when it hit. And it had hit Gavin Whitecross hard.

The door opened and a uniformed officer strolled in, followed by Methven. She gave a warm smile. 'Hi, Mr White-cross, my name is Tracy Scott. I'm a Family Liaison Officer. I see they've got you a cup of tea.' Another warm smile. 'I think I can rustle up some biscuits. Any particular favourites?'

'I'm fine, thanks.'

Methven motioned for them to join him in the corridor.

'This is where you tell me you've got something.' He was staring hard at Bain. 'Well?'

'Nothing much, Col. Boy's maybe hiding something, but I'm not the type to try and prise it out of him.'

Methven stared at him like he knew that was utter bollocks. 'Come on, gentlemen, let's see how Rachel's getting on.'

~

ON THE OTHER side of the glass, Dr Gibson dumped a mound of human organs onto a set of scales.

Time was Cullen would definitely lose his breakfast for the second time that morning just at the sight of it, but he'd seen so many dissections now. The stench from the bin, though... That was still new. He rested against the wall, feeling the tickle at the back of his throat.

'Well I fuckin' never.' Bain was messing about on his phone. 'So, a scaffie is short for "scavenger".'

Methven folded his arms and wouldn't look at them, instead keeping his focus on Dr Gibson working away through the glass. 'It's Doric. I spent five years up in Grampian, as you well know.'

'How the hell am I supposed to remember that, Col? Your boss punted me through here way before you pitched up. Almost like you got my job, eh?'

'We all remember why you were sent through here.'

Bain gave him a sharp look, but kept his peace for once.

A rap on the glass and they all looked round. Dr Gibson was standing over Paul Skinner's body, thumbing over to the door.

'Let's see what she's got for us, then?' Methven led them over.

The door was like an airlock on a submarine, a giant metal thing designed to keep any and all foreign forensic traces out of the post mortem. A loud hiss and Dr Gibson walked out, tugging her mask away from her face. 'Well.'

Bain wrapped his hands around his throat. 'So, death by the old Motherwell cuddle, aye?'

'Well. I'm not so sure.'

Methven frowned. 'Explain.'

'Initial blood toxicology shows a lot of alcohol in his system, but there's also a substantial amount of cocaine.'

'Cocaine.' Methven blew air up his face. 'Typical.'

'And I believe he was having sex at or near the time of death. Anal sex, too given the traces of condom spermicide on his penis and in his own anus. He'd worn protection and so did whoever had sex with him.'

Bain sniffed. 'Well, the boy was married to a bloke.'

But it got Cullen thinking. In this day and age, a lot more gay men were on anti-HIV medicine. He couldn't remember the name of it, but it let them forego protection, instead putting them at the mercy of less-fatal infections while they had their fun.

Bain was frowning. 'See with gay sex, is it like innings in cricket? "You go first, old chap."' He minced around a bit, arms waving. '"No, no, I insist, you first." That about right?'

The only sound was the jangling of Methven's change in his pocket.

The side door opened with the sound of flushing coming from the bathroom. McCrea walked out, drying his hands on his trousers. 'What's up?'

Methven ignored him. 'What I don't get is why Mr Skinner was trussed up in a nappy like one of McCrea's rape victims.'

'Hey, I didn't rape them!'

'You know what I mean.'

Cullen put his hands in his pockets and let out a deep breath. 'I can think of a good reason someone would murder him.'

'Go on?'

'Well, if his husband found him cheating, that'd be as good a motive as any. Right?'

Methven seemed to think it through. Jangle, jangle, jangle. Cullen wanted to force each bloody coin down his throat. 'Okay, take him in for an interview.'

5

Cullen hated bringing a grieving spouse in for a formal interview while their loved one's body was cut up and dissected on a slab in the pathology lab.

'Interview commenced at 11.57.' Bain sat back and folded his arms. 'Could you start with the last time you saw your husband, please.'

Whitecross took a deep breath. 'Breakfast yesterday morning.'

'I take it you have a job?'

'I'm a corporate lawyer.' And yet he'd not brought a criminal defence solicitor in. Could mean everything, could mean nothing. 'I was busy all day at work. Never rains but it pours. Locked in meetings, working through contracts and I didn't have anything to eat since my morning porridge.'

'Did you hear from your husband at all?'

'A few texts, you know how it is.' And Cullen did, but his own phone had been quiet since first thing. 'Paul called about three, maybe half past. I could check?'

'Let's do that later. What did he say?'

'Paul and his business partner closed a big deal yesterday and were going out to celebrate. He was in the back of the taxi, as it happens. Asked if I wanted to join them.'

Cullen leaned forward in his chair. Something concrete started to form. 'And did you?'

'As much as I wanted to, I just needed to get home. Have a bath, then watch something on Netflix with a bottle of wine and a Chinese.'

'Did Paul say where they were going?'

'Byres Road, I think. Maybe that restaurant where they wear kilts. Paul has *such* a thing for them.'

'And you didn't join them?'

'No, I had my bath, watched two episodes of *Unbelievable*, then went to bed around eleven.'

'When did you notice your husband wasn't home?'

'I went to the toilet in the middle of the night. Must've been about two?' Whitecross tapped the black smartwatch on his wrist. 'Again, I could check?'

'That's okay for now.'

Whitecross seemed to relax.

'We will need to take it into evidence afterwards.' Cullen got the reaction he wanted. Slight fury at being inconvenienced. 'We may settle for access to any cloud service which houses the data.'

'Fine. Whatever.'

'So you've been awake since you noticed?'

'I, uh, went back to sleep.'

'Interesting.'

'Why?'

Cullen shrugged, but kept quiet. Let Whitecross break the silence.

'I presume there's a reason we're in an interview room instead of my home?'

Cullen nodded slowly. 'Your husband's post mortem revealed that he'd recently had sex with someone.'

Whitecross shut his eyes. 'I see.'

'Was it you?'

'I was at home, like I said.'

'You didn't answer the question.'

'No, it wasn't me. Christ. If you must know, I masturbated when I got in.'

Cullen noted it down. Hard to check unless it'd been to some internet porn. Another job for Elvis. 'You any idea who your husband might have had sex with?'

More silence, just the ticking of the clock on the wall over his head.

'Mr Whitecross, your husband's dead. We believe someone murdered him. I really want to find out who. If there's something you're not telling me, then I need to hear it. Whatever it is.'

Whitecross stared at him, his eyes ringed by tears. As much as Cullen hated doing this to a grieving man, there was a murderer out there. Maybe it was McCrea's rapist and he'd escalated to murder, maybe not. But Cullen wanted to catch him.

Whitecross ran a hand down his face. 'As much as we love each other and are committed to the life we've built together, it's quite common that one of us doesn't come home. Paul and I have an open relationship.'

Bain raised his eyebrows. 'I see.'

Whitecross tilted his head back. 'What is that supposed to mean?'

'Just sayin', pal. You need to be careful in this day and age.'

'What's that supposed to mean?'

'Nothing.'

'I get it. You're talking about HIV.'

Bain snarled, like he could catch it from sitting in the same room as a gay man. Time was, a lot of people would share that stupid idea. Bain seemed old enough to remember Princess Diana holding that ailing man's hand, to remember the furore, to remember nothing happening to her, to remember a dark time when homophobes ran the world.

Maybe the world wasn't so much better now.

'Paul and I are both on PrEP.'

Bingo. That was the name.

Bain was frowning, though. Hard to believe someone as depraved as him wouldn't know. Maybe he was playing the daft laddie. 'What's that when it's at home?'

'It's a pill you take that protects you against HIV. And besides, AIDS isn't the death sentence it was when I came out.'

Cullen shot a glare at Bain, then gave Whitecross a smile. 'Sir, do you have any idea who your husband was sleeping with last night?'

'You mean who he fucked?' Whitecross dabbed at his eyes. 'I hate euphemisms. But no, I don't know where Paul slept last night, or who he fucked or who fucked him.'

'You said he was out on the randan with his business partner?' Bain folded his arms across his chest.

Whitecross sat there, like he was waiting for a question. 'Excuse me?'

'Well, could your husband have... you know... with them?'

'Iain Farrelly is his name, and no; he's extremely heterosexual.'

Cullen kicked Bain's ankle to shut him up. 'You got a name or address for Mr Farrelly?'

'Not a home address, no. Iain and Paul have an office on Blythswood Square.'

Bain leaned over to whisper to Cullen: 'Want me to head round there?'

Now he'd decided to play the enthusiastic underling. Cullen shook his head, mindful of Dr Gibson's lack of certainty over the cause of death. 'Let's speak to Methven first.'

Upstairs in Govan station, Cullen opened the door and realised he'd been in this office before, looking across the wasteland that was southern Glasgow. Half a mile away, an Asda glowed in the morning gloom next to the Rangers football stadium, floodlights on full to help the midwinter grass grow. He shut the office door behind him. 'Any update from the PM?'

Methven sat behind the desk and joined Cullen in staring out across the cityscape. 'Not yet.'

'So what do you want us to do, sir?'

'I've thought about your update from the interview. We

should get some bodies round to the Blythswood Square office and see what this business partner has to say for themself.'

'Him, sir. Name is Iain Farrelly.' Cullen flicked open his notebook. 'Sounds like their business is specialising in data integration. Whatever that is.'

Now Methven looked round. 'It's a real growth industry. Remember that case at Alba Bank a while back?'

'What about it?' Cullen shuddered, remembering it all in vivid detail. 'They weren't working there, were they?'

'No, but a competitor was.' Methven sighed. 'I spent a very long hour listening to the CEO expounding on it. He was a suspect as— Well. It's a lucrative business, let's just leave it at that.'

'So we should progress a financial explanation for his murder?'

Methven nodded. 'It's possible. And if it's been happening, there could be demands. Emails, letters, anything.'

'I'll get someone on it, sir.'

'Think that's a waste of time, Col.' Bain sniffed. 'Way I see it, the boy was gay, right? Had an open relationship. Stands to reason he'd go out looking for some trade. Maybe he found it, had a bit of how's your father in that lane, and the wee scrote swiped his wallet, emptied it and dumped it.'

'Okay, Brian, get a few officers going door to door in the lane, see what you can dig up.'

Bain beamed, but didn't say anything.

Methven looked round at Cullen. 'How does that sound to you, Scott?' Always a challenge with him, always playing people off against each other.

'I agree we should devote some resources to that. The body was found there, so we might find some lead that points to whoever dumped it. But given the lack of forensics or blood trail, it looks like Skinner was just dropped there. Meaning he was killed elsewhere. The bleach points to someone having half a clue as to how to lose any evidence linking them to a corpse.'

Methven jangled his coins and keys hard, thinking it all through. 'So the culprit stole a wallet, strangled the victim, stripped him naked, put a nappy on him? And how heavy is a body to lift into the dumpster?'

'Sir, I'm just saying how I see it. It's likely he was killed elsewhere, then transported here.'

'And our killer conveniently had a few gallons of bleach to hand?'

Cullen could only shrug. 'The bleach points to someone having half a clue as to how to lose any evidence linking them to a corpse. I think we need to put our eggs in a few baskets. Yes, we might get lucky around here but someone could've bought a ton of bleach in one go, for instance. You never know.'

Bain sat there, arms folded.

'You disagree with me, Sergeant?'

Bain sucked in a breath. 'Think if we don't go in there with all hands, then we might lose something central to this. No CCTV, so we need anything we can get from the crime scene.'

'I'm just saying that we've got twenty officers bombing along the M8 just now. I don't want to allocate them all to one place. We need to cast our net wide.'

Methven got up and walked over to the window. 'Brian, can you get on top of searching the immediate vicinity for me?'

'You wanting to split me and Sundance up here? That it?'

'I don't want you two running around while my street team is a gang of headless chickens, do I?'

6

BAIN

Back at the crime scene now. A ton of uniforms here, and no bugger's supervising them. Could've sworn McCrea should be doing this, but that wee bugger's got a habit of clearing off when there's work to be done.

A car pulls up nearby and here they are, Tweedledumb and Tweedledumber. Sure I must've used that line before, but sod it. Still funny and it's never been more fuckin' apt than right now.

Elvis is first out of the car, lugging a laptop under his arm like he always does. Not a bad lad, but people like Cullen and Methven only use him to do their donkey work, means he keeps down at that level. CCTV, telephony, that kind of shite. Not like we don't have whole departments for it. 'Morning, Bri.'

I set over and—Christ alive—big Craig Hunter gets out the driver side. Sundance's old mate. Still acts like a squaddie, got that sharp-eyed look, twitching and scanning around like there's a sniper waiting in every window.

So I just stop dead, let that prick come to me. 'Morning, lads.'

Elvis joins us by the motor. Knows not to touch it.

Hunter though, rests his big mitts against it when he leans back. 'You boys still recording your podcast?'

What the hell? That cheeky bastard. 'What podcast?'

'The Crafty Butcher featuring Elvis and the Billy Boy. Right?'

Tell you, Hunter's getting it, and both fuckin' barrels. I'm right in his face, but the prick's about a foot taller than us. 'How the fuck did you find out?' A wee bit of spit sprays out of my mouth and covers his jacket.

Elvis gets a big scowl, but he's not looking at me.

Hunter looks down at us. 'My old man's a big fan.'

'Forgot about that big deviant. Makes me sick thinking of what he's sticking his cock into while he listens.'

That's got him. He's shut up, but he's glowering at us like he's going to smash my head off the pavement.

So I break off. Hunter'll keep for later. 'Come on, let's go over and see what's what.' I lead the pair of arseholes over the road and sign the pricks in. Boy managing the crime scene could give Hunter a run for his money in the old big bastard stakes.

Then a smurf-suited figure comes over, clutching a phone to his bonce. 'Aye, aye, just be over.' He pulls his mask down. McCrea, sneaky wee bastard. 'Alright, gaffer?'

'Had better ones. Where you off to?'

'Johnny Napier said my breath smelled, and I had onions at breakfast. Just had a mint. Don't want to be speaking to any flighty witness with onion breath, eh?' McCrea blows across my puss. 'Do I smell?'

'Jesus, get away from you, you daft sod. Where are you going?'

Prick frowns. 'Right, well. DI Cullen told me to head off to investigate Gavin Whitecross.' So McCrea's sooking up to Sundance? 'Reckons I can give the local gen, so what can I say?'

'How about "piss off"?'

But he's walking away to dump his suit in the discard pile. 'Catch you later.'

I'll try and not let that faze us any. So I clap my hands

together. 'A body was dumped here. It's possible he was murdered nearby, or elsewhere. Either way, I want to know. DC Gordon, can you get on top of telephony and CCTV?'

Elvis gives us a sigh. And I feel like a right arsehole. All those chats in annual review meetings with Sundance and Crystal Methven have clearly fallen on deaf ears with yours truly. 'Fine.' Looks anything but, like, but what can you do? Needs must and all that.

'Hunter, can you—'

'Gaffer?' McCrea's back over *sans* his crime scene suit. Boy's porked out since we worked together, that's for sure. 'Forgot to say. This lassie came down.' He points up at the flats overlooking the lane. 'Said she lives up there might've seen someone dumping the body.'

~

THE LASSIE'S BIG LIKE. Taller than me, though not as big as that lassie who came back. What's her name? Caldwell, that's it. Aye, her. Hair's still damp from a shower, but not that wet that she's just got out. Wearing a tracksuit like she's going out for a run. But after a shower? Doesn't hang together, if you ask me. Not that she's showing us in.

Anyway, I'm hanging back and letting Hunter take charge.

'So I gather you saw someone last thing yesterday?'

'That's right.' She keeps looking at us. And I know what it is: that fuckin' boil on my conk. Hurts to touch, and I keep wanting to touch the fuckin' thing. She guides us into the flat, then kinda floats over the stripped-wood flooring.

Nice pad in here, have to say. All IKEA by the looks of it, but not the cheapest stuff. Big sofa, coffee table full of shite, and a cracking telly hanging on the wall.

She takes Hunter over to the window, but I'm distracted by the telly. It's paused, with some lassie I know but can't place. Sometimes that's the kind of detail that'll crack a case. Never mind. I'll sort that later, so I join them by the window.

Actually looks like a professional outfit down there. Few SOCOs milling about, them arc light thingies blaring away, few bodies. Thank god I'm not on the hook for it, though, as there's a few too many of them pissing about. But then again, Sundance is the kind of guy who'll pin any blame on me. And Crystal's the kind who'll spread blame around like jam on a cake.

The factories behind are busy, likes. One's a brewery and there's all sorts of steam coming out. Might have to head in and sample their wares sometime.

But she's pointing at the bins. 'It was right down there. He lifted something up and tipped it in the bin.'

'You see what it was?'

'Might've been a carpet?' She shrugs at him and he's buying it wholesale. 'Why, what's going on down there?'

'Just wondering if you can give us a better description, that's all.'

'I saw a big guy running away from the lane. It was pitch black, so I didn't see much.' Her eyes switch between the both of us. 'You need to tell me what's happened here.'

Right, time for yours truly to step in. 'You mean big like DC Hunter here?'

'Maybe.' She gives us a sulky look. 'I don't know. Sorry.'

'What about compared with the officers you spoke to down at the crime scene?'

'Not really.'

Hunter looks over at us and I give him the tiniest shrug, so he smiles at her. 'Thanks for your time.'

❧

HUNTER HOLDS the stairwell door open for us. 'But she said he wasn't obese like DC McCrea.'

'He's not that bad.' Though I give him a sneaky wee grin as we head back over to the motors. 'When I managed him, I saw his medical records... Man alive.' That hits us hard, can't help laughing at my own gag. 'Well, that man might not be alive much longer, have to say.'

'Is that supposed to be funny?'

'You can't deny that it's—'

'Look, *Sarge*, it was dark. She says she didn't see much more than an outline.'

Big man rushing away... What if it was a fat bastard like McCrea?

Well, the gears in my noggin have kicked into a much higher gear now. I stop by the cars and peer in. 'Elvis, did you finish that check for us?'

'What check?' Hunter's face is tripping him. 'Cullen know you're allocating work behind his back?'

'I'm all about the results, so let's see what's what before I pass on the good news to our fuckin' lord and master.' I give Elvis an opening. Prick doesn't pick up on it. So I clear my throat. 'Well, did you check on Big Jim for me?'

'Aye, did it while Hunter drove us through from Edinburgh.' Elvis unlocks that infernal laptop of his and checks the screen. 'One James Michael Bell, AKA Big Jim, the boy who found your body. Lives in Anniesland. Got a location on his phone at or near his home all last night.'

I expected better from Elvis. I thought Big Jim was a suspect I could haul over the coals, show Sundance and Crystal a fuckin' thing or two. Bust his alibi apart. 'Can you do us a solid, Elvis? Go up to flat nineteen and speak to the lassie. Show him a photo of this James Bell boy.'

He actually pricks up at that. Good boy. 'Cheers, Bri.' Laptop under his arm, and off he goes.

Hunter isn't so pleased. Fuckin' Harry Potter without the specs, away to grass on us to fuckin' Dumbledore Cullen.

'Come on, Craigie boy, it's fine.'

'It's not fine.' Hunter huffs out a sigh. 'Who is this James Bell anyway?'

'The binman who found the body. Him and the South African boy.' And I slip him the famous Bain grin. 'Thing is, he told us he was with a mate.'

Lights go on behind his eyes. Now he gets it. 'Okay. So you think he could've left his phone at home while he went elsewhere and killed Skinner?'

'Exactly.'

Hunter nods slowly. 'Let's pay him a visit then.'

∾

I PULL up my chariot by the portacabin and get out into the air. Even by the dump, it smells a fuckton better than back through in Edinburgh.

No sign of that clown Hunter, though. He'll be lucky to get two minutes before I head in there.

The depot's fuckin' buzzing. Boys everywhere, hopping down off lorries and making a nuisance of themselves with the queue of cars full of punters looking to drop off all the shite of the day at the recycling tip.

The passenger door slides open and Hunter gets in without asking. Wide bastard. 'I've been thinking it through as I drove over here.'

'Another way that you're as bad as fuckin' Sundance. Go on.'

'Do you have to swear so much?'

'Ever since I stopped smoking, aye. So what have you been thinking about, princess?'

'I can't follow your logic. Why would a binman dump a body?'

'Easy. You hear about these rapes McCrea's been working on?'

'Well, I was in the sexual offences unit until recently.'

'What did they do you for? Kiddie porn?'

'You know what I mean.' And I know how fuckin' funny I am. 'The SO unit is split up like the rest of Police Scotland. North, East, West. The Glasgow lot in West had us through for the sixth or seventh one, to cast an independent eye on their evidence. As far as I could tell, their investigation was sound. Trouble was, whoever was doing it was good. Knew how to cover their tracks.'

'Tell you, I blame that *CSI* shite on the telly. Half the fuckin' country knows how to cover their tracks like an expert.'

'So yes, I'm well aware of what's been going on through here.'

'Great. Well, this Big Jim boy found one of the victims. Lassie in Partick, been drugged, raped, stuck in a nappy and dumped in a bin.'

'Sarge.' Prick says it all sarcastic like, and he's wincing. 'You need to do your homework. Except for her, the victims were all male. Rapists playing both sides of the tracks are extremely rare, except when they prey on children.'

Wanker.

'Either way, someone matching this Big Jim's description is seen fleeing the dumping site? Stands to reason he's a suspect.'

Hunter's fuckin' understanding it now. 'You think the perp's escalated to murder?'

'Stands to reason, right?'

'So why own up to discovering the body?'

He's got us.

But sing hosanna if that South African boy doesn't mince past right then. Even in the pissing rain he's topless. What a lad. 'Because his mate there interrupted it, eh? Big Jim's plan was to not find the body, but instead stick the body in the back of the lorry. Turn it to mincemeat and dump it in the wilds. Even if someone finds the body, they've no idea which bin it's come from. Right?'

'So you think this is him slipping up?'

'Right. Boy's a sex pest. Clocked him ogling some school-girls earlier.'

A rap at the glass and some big bastard's staring in, gurning at us. Ah, it's Big Jim. A thumb lets him know he can get in the back. The plastic sheets are still down from the Duchess's last MOT, so a binman is in.

Have to stifle a laugh when I think about Sundance and his scaffie. Christ, they breed them different up there, that's for sure.

Hunter's glaring at us. And he's got the look of someone who's taken a life. 'We should do this in a station.'

'Bollocks to that.' I swivel round and give the boy the evils. 'Thanks for meeting us, sir.'

'Don't mention it.'

'Well done for admitting to finding the body. For calling it in. Lot of people wouldn't do that in this day and age.'

He shrugs. 'Just doing my public duty.'

'How about going one step further and admitting to putting it there?'

'What?' He's looking at Hunter like he's going to bail him out of this. 'This is bullshit!'

'Aye? You found the body, stands to reason you killed the guy too.'

'This is bollocks!'

I give him a few seconds, let him build up a head of steam. Can almost see it blowing out of the clown's ears. 'Your alibi doesn't stack up.'

'Of course it does.'

'Nope. See, you told us you were at a friend's house. Your phone was at home all that time.'

He just sniffs.

'You didn't take it?'

'No.' Takes him way too long to think it through. 'It was charging.'

'Why wouldn't you take your phone?'

'I'm not a prisoner to it. Christ.'

'You're going to be a prisoner to Her Majesty, though.'

Doesn't get the response I want. The prick laughs. And he's talking pish, he's got a fancy smartphone, stands to reason he'd be staring into it just like everyone else would.

'Come on, pal, just admit it. Then we'll all be done and home by teatime.'

And the big guy bursts into tears.

Hunter gives us a look like I made that happen. He reaches over and pats the guy on the shoulder. 'You okay?'

'The fuck do you think?' Big Jim sits back and his face is a mess. Red and blotchy, his lip quivering like it's epileptic. 'I found a dead body this morning!'

Hunter narrows his eyes at him. No matter what I say about him, he's good. Can spot a liar at a million miles. Need to give him a nickname, but Hunter's almost too fuckin' apt. 'How about you tell the truth?'

Big Jim stares at him for a few, then runs his tattooed wrist over his snotty nose. 'I was at a mate's house, playing cards.'

'Gambling?'

He nods. 'Reason I didn't take my phone is it was a pressie from my daughter.' Ah shite. The photo on his phone wasn't a victim of his, it was his daughter. 'Shelly's a good girl. I worked so hard to get her the best. She's a lawyer earns big money down in London. Done me so proud. Bought me that phone for my Christmas. I know how much it's worth. Cost like a grand and she pays the contract on it. I'm in so much debt to those boys, if they saw my phone, they'd take it right off us. Sell it to some shonky wee shop in Dumbarton.'

'Take it your debt's bigger than a grand?'

'Aye. Few times that. Can't not go for another card night, otherwise they'll break my legs. And I need to work.'

'So, this friend of yours got a name?'

'I can't tell you it!'

He gets a pointed finger from yours truly. 'Bud, you tell us or you're going down for murder. Your choice.'

7

CULLEN

Cullen walked along Blythswood Square, passing through crowds of workers carrying their lunches back to their offices. Hunger gnawed at his gut, but he didn't want to stop to eat, not while they had active leads.

The IP Consulting office was in a stone building that used to be a bank, judging by the ornate stonework above the door. Sometime in the last five years, it'd been hollowed out and turned into a shared office hub.

Cullen stepped over to the front door and checked his phone. No reply from McCrea, so he called him.

Answering the phone was the one thing McCrea did quickly. 'Whazzup?'

'Looking around, but I can't see you.'

'Soz, got caught up with the forensics lad. Running prints on your wallet.'

'Getting anything?'

'Aside from traces of bleach, I've got a used condom, an apple core and half a tin of ginger. Boy thinks Coke, but could be Pepsi. I've got a suspicion it's Dr Pepper.'

Cullen didn't know how he coped working in Edinburgh without such high quality officers as Damian McCrea... 'So it's a dead end?'

'Looks like it, aye.'

Cullen couldn't decide if someone dumping a wallet beside a body was a good thing or not. Were they careless? Arrogant? Or did they plan for the body to be collected and disposed of by the binmen? 'Got hold of Petersen's alibi yet?'

'Next on my list.'

Cullen sighed again. Becoming a habit, but then dealing with Damian McCrea was right up there with his career highlights. 'Can you do it, then get your arse over here, please?'

'Sure, *boss*.' And McCrea was gone.

Cullen pocketed his phone and got himself straight again. Adjusted his suit jacket, ran his hand through his hair. Ready. He opened the door and walked in.

A long desk ran along the far wall, but only one person looked like they were working reception. The other seats were all occupied by single people with headphones, tucking into boxed salads. In Glasgow. Two football tables were in use, four lads in their late teens working each one, the balls clanking and the handles rattling as they cheered and goaded each other.

The receptionist swanned over, looking like she was suffering from a fit of smiling. Mid-twenties, wearing tight jeans and a pink T-shirt stencilled with WorkPlace. 'Hey, can I help?' Her accent was a mix of Paisley and Brooklyn.

'Is this the IP Consulting office?'

'Second floor. Two offices upstairs on permanent lease.'

～

'DI Scott Cullen.' He showed his warrant card. 'This is DC McCrea. Looking to speak to Iain Farrelly?'

'Stuart McKendrick.' McKendrick seemed surprised by him being a cop. Not the first time Cullen had received that reaction, just one of those rare occasions he didn't use it to his advantage. But McKendrick looked like he needed to sleep, and not on his office floor like it seemed he'd done. Wild bed head hair, even wilder eyes hidden behind thick lenses. Checked shirt under a grey jumper with a logo Cullen didn't recognise, not that it hid his surprisingly large gut. The rest of him was stick thin, but his belly made him look pregnant. He held out a hand to shake, but only McCrea took him up on it. 'Come on in.'

His office was a glass-walled corner of the floor with a massive window looking back along the street to Cullen's car.

Cullen stayed by the door. 'So, is Mr Farrelly about?'

McKendrick sat behind a glass desk, but didn't seem too sure. 'He's not in today.'

'Oh?'

'Yeah. Only ever have a couple of staff here at any time, usually out on site somewhere.'

'What about you?'

'I'm the CFO.'

'Chief Financial Officer?' McCrea's lower jaw jutted open.

'That's right. Obviously I don't need to be on site, but the rest of the guys usually are. We have a development and testing capability, but again they're off today.'

'Any particular reason for this?'

'Well, Paul—he's the CEO—he gave them all the day off today. Big party last night.'

That all tallied with Gavin Whitecross's story, his tale of his husband's celebration after clinching a big deal.

'What was this party in aid of?'

'Well.' McKendrick yawned into his fist. 'Sorry, it's billing day. Means I've got to be in to process all the invoices otherwise everything goes to sh— sugar.'

'Anyway, can I speak to Mr Farrelly?'

'Oh, sure. I've got his home address somewhere. Let me have a quick look.' McKendrick opened a desk drawer and started rummaging around.

Cullen looked around the office. McKendrick was clearly a big Rangers fan, with a cabinet filled with memorabilia, not least a signed shirt with Hateley on the back, mounted on a legless dummy. Cullen turned back round to see what was keeping McKendrick.

He'd fallen asleep.

Cullen leaned over to prod him. 'Mr McKendrick?'

He jerked awake. '—not my problem!' He blinked hard a few times. 'Sorry, who the hell are you?'

'Police, sir. You were going to give me Mr Farrelly's home address?'

~

BEARSDEN WAS Glasgow's answer to Morningside, very well-to-do and upmarket, like its own little town inside the city limits.

Cullen got out of his car and leaned against the side, waiting.

Another Victorian villa but the other side of the city from Paul Skinner's Southside home. Music pumped out of an upstairs bedroom, in time to some disco lights. A dance remix of The Killers, that one about a sex change or whatever. Bet the neighbours loved this house.

His phone rang. Methven. He put it to his ear. 'What's up?'

'Do you have a mobile number for Jimmy Deeley?'

'He not answering his office phone?'

'He's on the golf course, as far as his assistant can tell. Need him through here to give a second opinion.'

'Dr Gibson will be happy with that.'

'It's at her insistence. Her colleagues through here are backed up with these murders, so I need to get hold of Jimmy. So do you have any other means of contacting him or am I completely wasting my time here?'

'I do, as it happens.'

A car door slammed behind Cullen. McCrea tugging his trousers out of his arse.

'Better go, sir. I'll text you his number.' Cullen ended the call and dug out Deeley's contact details, then sent them to Methven. He put his phone away and turned to McCrea. 'You took your time.'

'Sorry.' McCrea didn't look it, judging by his grin. 'You alright?'

'I've had better.' Cullen set off towards the house, storming up the path. He stopped and rapped on the door, doubting anyone inside could hear it over the music. 'You get anywhere with the alibi for Rich Petersen?'

'Aye.'

'And?'

'Still got a few things to check.'

'I take it that means you haven't got in touch with this Marie Gray, then?'

'Something like that.' McCrea shrugged. Upstairs, The Killers segued into Erasure and McCrea's fierce look softened. 'Love that tune, man.'

Thirty seconds since Cullen had knocked, and nobody had answered. Cullen walked across the pristine lawn to peer in through the front window.

Past a wall of pot plants, a man and a woman lounged back on an L-shaped Chesterfield, wearing dressing gowns. A Nintendo Switch rested on a duck-egg blue coffee table, and they were each holding a small grey controller, swaying as they played a game. Probably *Mario Kart*, if Cullen could guess. Dark, dark rings around their eyes. Hard to tell if they were a couple or just friends.

Cullen thumped the glass and waved.

They both jerked forward. The woman shot to her feet and hurried out of the room. The man covered his mouth, then reached for a smartphone next to the Switch. Erasure stopped playing, but the lights still flashed.

The front door had opened by the time Cullen trudged back over.

The woman stepped out onto the steps, barefoot, hugging her cream dressing gown tight. Dyed-blonde hair scraped back into a ponytail. Tanned skin, but from a bottle rather than natural sources. 'Can I help?' Broad Glasgow accent.

'DI Scott Cullen.' He held out his warrant card. 'And this is DC Damian McCrea. Need a word with an Iain Farrelly.'

'If it's about the noise, I can—'

'It's about Paul Skinner.'

That got a flick of eyebrows. A response, at least. 'Oh. Come on in, then.' She slipped inside the house, her bare feet slapping across the stripped wooden flooring, then into the living room. Wooden skirting to match the floors, stark white walls. Four pot plants sat in galvanised buckets near the window.

Iain Farrelly looked like a fat potato stuffed into a silk gown. Ginger hair softened by silver streaks. He frowned at Cullen's warrant card. 'Oh Christ.' Sounded like he was Australian, with an outside chance of being a New Zealander. 'What's going on?'

Cullen stayed standing, while McCrea perched on an armchair. 'Mr Farrelly, we need to talk to you about Paul Skinner. Gavin Whitecross told us you and Mr Skinner are business partners?'

'That's right. We co-own IP Consulting.'

'And when was the last time you saw him?'

'Last night.'

'Where and with whom?'

'A few guys from work, at a restaurant in the West End.' Farrelly swallowed hard. 'What's happened?'

'Mr Skinner is dead.'

'Oh Christ.' Farrelly shut his eyes and his shoulders sagged. His face screwed up tight. Seemed like a genuine show of grief rather than playacting. And Cullen had seen both enough times to know the difference. 'What happened?'

'We believe he was murdered. Strangulation. How did he seem last night?'

'Good. We, uh, closed a deal yesterday, selling sixty percent of the business to a big firm. Golden handcuffs for three years then we get a premium for the other forty percent. We took the team out for dinner, then a few of us came back here for a small party.'

'Can you name the attendees?'

'Well, there was me and Paul. Er, look I'm not that comfortable sharing this with you.'

'Was Gavin Whitecross here?'

'Gav? No.'

'Well, Mr Skinner is undergoing a post mortem just now. Anything you want to own up to, now's the time.'

Farrelly just shook his head.

Cullen's phone rang. Elvis. With a sigh, Cullen got up. 'Better take this.' He nodded to McCrea to take over, then walked into the hall. 'Elvis, you got something?'

'Under the bloody cosh, Craig.'

'It's Scott. You did mean to call me?'

'Aye, right. Sure. Sorry, Scott, I was just speaking to Craig and my wires are a wee bit crossed. You boys sure know how to ride me hard.'

Cullen looked back through, but it didn't look like McCrea was getting anything more out of Farrelly. 'What have you got for me?'

'Just got the phone records through. Apols for the delay, but the network were being twats. Looks like Skinner was at an address in Bearsden.'

Cullen nodded. Right where he was now. 'You got the same for Whitecross?'

'I used to go out with a lassie from Bearsden when I was at uni, dirty as hell.' Keyboard sounds in the background. 'Yup, Whitecross was at home from seven, or his phone was anyway.'

'Shite. You're sure?'

'Afraid so. Round there just now. Got one of those Ring cameras just like half the world does. Got the credentials and it shows Whitecross getting home and not leaving until the morning. I mean, he could've turned it off, but it was backed it up with activity on his Netflix account. Did that thing where the autoplay asks if there's anyone still there and he was. The telly in their front room was playing two episodes of *Unbelievable*. Damn good show, that.'

'So he was at home. Bugger. Cheers, Elvis. That's good work.' Cullen ended the call and gave himself a few seconds to figure it all out.

So Whitecross was telling the truth. He'd been at home while his husband was out playing. And his husband had been right here.

Assuming he'd picked someone up at this party, they'd either killed him or had a bloody good idea who had.

But if he'd left alone, then maybe he'd gone somewhere. A

gay bar maybe, met someone there. Or the same on Grindr or, like Bain suggested, found someone on the street.

Either way, they'd drawn a blank on Whitecross. Maybe Bain and Hunter would get lucky with their side of the coin, but Cullen needed answers on who was at the party, so he headed to the lounge.

McCrea was coming back from the kitchen with two steaming mugs of coffee. He leaned in to whisper: 'Just plunged it and it's a two-litre job. You want one?'

'No.'

McCrea rested the cups either side of the Switch. 'Here you go.'

'Cheers.' The woman took hers and held it up, soaking in the aroma.

'Thanks.' Farrelly didn't take his. 'I can't believe this. Paul was right here.'

Cullen took his seat again. 'Mr Farrelly, I need to know who was here. Okay?'

'Fine. Paul and I, plus a few people from our senior team. Dave H, David F, John, Keith. Oh, and Stuart.'

Cullen had seen first-hand the state Stuart had got into. 'Anyone seem particularly friendly with Mr Skinner?'

'Not that I can think of. I mean, they're all married. Not that that stops that kind of thing, I guess.'

'So it was just yourself, two Davids, a John, a Keith and a Stuart?'

'Well, Marie came home at about eleven with her pal. As usual, she stuck on the tunes and we had some fun.'

McCrea leaned forward on his armchair, frowning. 'What's your surname?'

She twisted her lips into a pout. 'Gray?'

Confusion clouded Cullen's head like a hangover in a post-session sleep. Then it clicked. He knew who Marie was now. Rich Petersen's alibi. 'See, I've been trying to phone a Marie Gray all morning. You know a Rich Petersen?'

She nodded. 'We were out for some cocktails, then we came back here.'

Cullen felt the confusion clouding him again. None of it made any sense now. 'Mr Petersen found Paul Skinner's body.'

She covered her mouth with a hand. 'What?'

Cullen's heart was thudding in his chest. He tried to play it cool, but everything screamed in his head. 'Did you see him speaking to Paul Skinner?'

'Well, yeah. They went home together.'

8

Bain

I chuck the balled-up wrapper out the window and take a glug from the bottle of WakeyWakey. Smashing chips. Only downside is choosing the small bag.

Trouser pocket, front right. Phone's not fuckin' there. Shite.

Suit jacket pocket. Thank fuck. Did not want to have to hunt this bugger. I hit up Hunter and he answers. Nice when someone respects a hierarchy. Years of being in the army did that to the poor bugger. Sounds like he's not driving like I hoped he'd be. 'Where are you?'

'Dalmarnock.'

'What the fuck are you doing there, you dope?'

'Verifying Big Jim's story. That's where the card game was.'

'With you now. You getting anything?'

'It's not him, Brian. He's got a nails alibi.'

Fuck's sake. Big Jim was my number one suspect. 'Spill.'

'He was here all night. Got him on street CCTV outside the house. Arrived at nine, left about two in the morning. Unless he climbed out of a third-floor window and shimmied down, he was there all that time.'

'The size of that boy, the only thing he's climbing is the walls in Bar-L when I get him for kiddy fiddling. Craig, mosey on back to the station, I'll meet you there.' I kill his call and see a text from Elvis:

Jane Munro in that flat. Definitely not matching Big Jim's description.

Aye, no fuckin' shit. Would've been useful to know that before I sent Hunter round on that wild fuckin' goose chase.

Phone's ringing again, so I hold it out to see who's calling. Sundance. Never gives up, does he? Giving him another promotion just made him even worse. Acting DI. Acting Dead Important more like.

Switch over. 'What's up, Sundance?'

'Where are you?'

'Getting something to eat. That Hunter boy... Never seen anyone eat so slowly as him. Takes him hours to eat a slice of bread, I swear.'

'Is Hunter with you?'

Another glug of WakeyWakey. That's the ticket! 'He's making himself useful.'

'Where?'

'Never you mind.'

'I'm not in the mood.'

Never fuckin' are, but I don't say that. 'He's just spoken to some boys about a card school. Turns out that Big Jim lad is up to his conkers in debt. He's not our guy. Solid alibi.'

'I know. It's why I've been trying to speak to you! Paul Skinner was last seen with Rich Petersen.'

'What?' Sounds like it's time to start up the Duchess and get round there.

'Your sexy binman is—'

'I fuckin' told you to—'

'Brian, I need you to head to his home address. I texted you it. Okay?'

'On my way.' A cheeky look at the display while Sundance rabbits on. I know the place. Just round the corner. 'Where are you?'

'I'm at the bin depot.'

'We were just there.' Stop at the junction, indicating right and the glass in my boot rattles. 'There's a smashing wee micro-brewery down the road from there. Stocked up on some bottles.'

'McCrea's on his way over. Get hold of Hunter and use them as back up, okay?'

'Probably caught up in traffic. I'll head in when I get there.'

'Wait for Hunter and McCrea!'

'You saying I can't arrest some wee arsehole? Piss off.'

'Stay and wait.'

'What was that?' I kill the call. Cheeky bastard. Acting Deaf and Ignorant now.

9

CULLEN

Cullen pulled up in the recycling centre car park, wedged between a load of ageing Audis, BMWs and Volkswagens. Old, most likely predating the introduction of electronics into motors, turning them more into computers than machines, the kind of cars you could still fix yourself.

Like everything in Glasgow, the recycling centre was three times the size of its Edinburgh equivalent, like the massive IKEA he'd seen signs for. That place was huge, big enough that they still had stock when Edinburgh ran out. Cullen had made that trip a few times, usually against his will. Not even the promise of a plate of meatballs and chips could make up for it.

He got out into the thin rain.

Rich Petersen was the last person seen with Paul Skinner. The one who found his body. All this time they'd focused on Gavin Whitecross and Big Jim. All along, it'd been the other man who'd discovered the body.

Right?

A bin lorry hurtled past, two men hanging off the back,

gloved hands clutching on tight. Looked like extreme sports types.

Cullen clocked a guy who looked like a foreman standing by a metallic grey box, the corner roof turned up like a hipster's haircut. His acid yellow safety jacket screamed into the brief flash of sunshine. The supervisor, judging by the green stencilling on his jacket, wandering over, pulling his gloves off. 'Can't park there, bud.'

'DI Scott Cullen.' He held up his warrant card, long enough for the bloke to read every single character on there and process each dot that made up his photograph. 'Need a word with Rich Petersen.'

'Davie Parrott.' He thrust out a hand, so mucky that it was like he hadn't bothered with the gloves. 'I'm his supervisor.'

Cullen didn't take it, instead putting his warrant card away. 'Is he here?'

'Nah, buggered off home about an hour ago. Said he couldn't cope with the stress. First time he's found a body.'

'Been a few, though, right?'

'Happens once every couple years. Found three bodies myself in a fortnight. Weren't related, either. Freakiest thing.' He tugged the work glove back on. 'You talking about the lassie Big Jim found out in Partick, right?'

'Maybe.'

'Jim's a bit of a deviant, but his heart's in the right place. His daughter's a good girl, he couldn't help but think it was her.' He grimaced. 'Weird business, that. Wait, you think Richie topped the boy him and Jim found?'

Cullen smiled, trying not to set off any warnings. 'Just got a few follow-up questions to ask. He a good worker?'

'Good enough.' Parrott blew air up his face. 'Shame about that topless shite, but what can you do?' He shook his head. 'You need his address?'

'Already got it. I'll head there now.' Cullen set off back towards his car and called Bain.

Engaged.

It just rang and rang. He tried McCrea's number again.

Answered straight away. 'Afternoon, gaffer.'

'You at the address yet?'

McCrea belched down the line. 'Sorry, had a black pudding supper. Big mistake. Repeating on me like an all-you-can-eat buffet.'

'Are you there?'

'Aye. Traffic's a shambles. No sign of Bain, though.'

'Can you see his car?'

'Oh, aye. No mistaking that beauty.'

Cullen started running. The daft bastard had gone inside on his own. 'I'll be there in two minutes. Hang tight.' He tried Bain again.

Still engaged. Everything felt wrong with that.

10

BAIN

That sexy binman boy's inside, I fuckin' know it. And now I'm working for fuckin' Sundance and he won't me let me go in on my jack. Fuckin' changed days, I tell you. Time was I was telling that prick what to do, now he's got the pips. Wanker.

But he's right. I shouldn't pile in there. Might be disco muscles the boy's blessed with, but sometimes pricks like that know a few more martial arts than mine: the ancient Glaswegian art of Fuh Kyu. Headbutts, knees to the knackers, cheeky bit of hair tugging.

No sign of McCrea or Hunter.

Phone's ringing.

Check all my pockets and my phone's not in any of them. Christ! It's slipped out the right side, stuck between the door and the seat. Bloody hell.

Hunter's calling.

So I answer. 'You on your way over?'

'I'm just about at the station.'

'I texted you! Get over here.'

Cheeky bugger tuts. 'You should've called me.'

'Just get your arse over here. Pronto.'

'I'll be ages with this traffic.'

And I catch sight of Petersen inside the flat. Prick is in his bedroom, stuffing clothes and shite into a bag. Packing to leave. 'Hurry.'

I open the door and get out onto the street.

Fuck Sundance, fuck Methven, fuck the lot of them.

This cunt's going down. Now.

11

CULLEN

Petersen lived in a council flat in Craigton, a cream box of misery, downwind from the crematorium. Cullen got out onto the street. The crematorium wasn't burning just now, so the street just stank of dog shit and fumes from a nearby factory, not that he could see any likely culprits.

McCrea was lurking in a doorway out of the rain, tucking into a fish supper. He crunched at a chunk of golden haddock. 'Scott.' Or at least it sounded like that through the white and beige mush.

'No sign of him?'

'Nope.' McCrea bit into a chip. 'Sorry, I was starving. Actually, not sure why I'm apologising to you.'

'Thought you'd had a black pudding supper?'

McCrea shrugged. 'Got hungry again, didn't I?'

'Right, finish that, then follow me.' Cullen walked over to the flat door and hit the buzzer.

No answer. He tried again, same result.

He stepped back and checked his phone. Still nothing from

Bain. He called him again. The faintest ringtone whispered out nearby.

Shite.

'Come fill up my cup, come fill up my can.'

Sounded like *Bonnie Dundee* by the Corries, the crowd clapping along in waltz time.

'Come saddle my horses and call out my men.'

Cullen followed the sound to a downstairs window, open to a thin crack. The blinds were drawn. He tried to open it further but it didn't budge.

'Unhook the West Port and let us gae free...'

The singing was louder over here. He tried to at least pull the blinds to the side, but he couldn't get his fingers through the crack.

'For it's up with the bonnets o' Bonnie Dundee.'

Cullen ran back to the tenement door. No sign of McCrea, either over the road or here. Brilliant.

What the hell could he do? Bain was inside the residence of a murder suspect.

Alone.

Petersen looked hard, ripped too. Bain was just attitude. He didn't stand a chance.

Cullen tried the doorknob and it opened into the stairwell. Two doors on the left, two on the right. "Petersen" was handwritten on a white card above the spyglass of the nearest. Cullen thumped the door. No answer.

Bugger it.

He launched himself at the door, shoulder first. It cracked open, and he tumbled through, sliding across shiny laminate. He picked himself up and snapped out his baton.

The flat was baking, like the thermostat was up to thirty. South African temperature. Two doors off the hallway, both hanging wide open.

Cullen hit dial on his phone again and Bain's ringtone chimed from the one on the left.

'Come fill up my cup, come fill up my can.'

Cullen stormed in and stopped dead.

A bedroom, the walls covered in pictures of musclebound

men and women. Bodybuilder types, all with shiny skin, posing and curling and whatever else they called it.

Bain lay on the bed, eyes rolling round in his head, naked except for a nappy.

Cullen raced over and crouched low. 'Are you okay?'

'Fuckin' never been better.' Bain pawed at him, like he thought Cullen was inches away rather than feet. 'I love you, big guy.'

Cullen got out his phone and called McCrea. 'Damian, where the hell are you?'

'Just chucking my wrapper in the bin.'

'Call an ambulance and get in here.'

'Sundance, I want to fuckin' have your little fuckin' babies!' Bain was staring at something over Cullen's shoulders, his eyes bulging.

Something blunt and hard hit Cullen in the shoulder. Felt like it'd torn open his old wound. He screamed and tumbled forward, landing on Bain. A swift kick hit his side.

Cullen tried to stand up, but Bain was clinging on to him. Something wet touched his neck. 'Mmm.'

A loud clatter came from the other room.

'Get off!' Cullen pushed away from Bain, then stumbled up to standing. He darted out into the hall. A rattle came from through the door. A living room with a tiny kitchen in the corner. The window was open, dirty yellow blinds flapping in the breeze.

Cullen raced in and clambered up onto the counter. He tore the blinds away from the wall so he could see out.

A patchy backyard, barely a garden, just damp dirt. Petersen was halfway up a brick wall at the back, climbing like a cat. Then he was on top, looking like he was going to drop down.

Cullen pushed through the window frame and dropped down onto hard ground.

Petersen glanced back the way he'd come. 'Aw, fuck!' He disappeared over the wall.

Cullen bombed it over the garden and jumped at the wall, grabbing the top and pulling himself up, feeling like his arms were going to tear. His shoulder gave way and he fell back into the mud. Luckily it was dirt, rather than dog shite, but another agonising jolt of pain ran up his collarbone.

A wheelbarrow was propped against the wall. He flipped it over and hopped onto the green metal. Let him get a run at the wall, hitting it at waist height, but at least he could see over.

Just a yard at the back of a factory. Machines hissed and roared inside. Some parked forklifts. A row of chunky wheelie bins lined the wall. A gang of workmen standing around eating from Greggs bags.

He vaulted over and landed on hard ground with a thud that juddered right up his spine. He scanned round for Petersen, his breath catching in his throat.

No sign of him.

Shite.

Where the hell was he?

Cullen jogged towards the workies, warrant card out. 'Police. Have you seen a man come this way?'

Just got shaking heads.

Bollocks.

Cullen took another look around. Where would he go? This was Petersen's territory, and Cullen was forty miles from home. Thirty miles from anywhere he knew.

Aha.

He stopped by the row of bins. 'I know you're in there.'

Nothing.

'I'll just search these, one by one.' He prodded the first one with his baton.

A sound came from the far end.

Cullen went over and shook it. 'Get out, now.'

'Fuck off!'

Cullen tried to wheel the bin out, but it was way too heavy.

It tipped over and Rich Petersen tumbled out in a pile of sawdust, his bare torso slicked with sweat and totally covered in residue.

Cullen held up his baton. 'Stay right there!'

But Petersen was halfway up, resting on hands and knees. 'Fuck off, mate.'

'I'm serious. Don't move!'

Petersen jerked up to standing and his left hand flashed forward. Pain seared Cullen's arm, biting into his aching shoulder and up his neck. His baton clattered to the ground. Something crunched at his foot, like someone had driven a bus over it. His scream sounded like it was someone else's. The pain was all his, coursing up his leg.

Petersen pushed him back against the bin, gripping both of Cullen's wrists tight.

Cullen struggled against him, but he was losing. Petersen was strong. Much stronger than Cullen.

Petersen swept his foot behind Cullen's knee and pushed him forward. Cullen slumped against the bin with a crack.

'Lie down!' Petersen held Cullen's baton in front of his face. 'I'm going to insert this—' He broke off, stepped away and raised the baton. 'Get the fuck away from me, man!'

McCrea stood next to him, holding his own baton like it was a golf club. 'Drop it.'

With his free hand, Petersen gave a come-on gesture. 'Just bring it. I can take you!'

'There's a ton of cops heading here, pal. You're getting—'

In a flash, Petersen caught McCrea's arm with Cullen's truncheon. McCrea's baton clattered to the ground, rolling towards the bin.

Cullen tried to inch forward to take it, but his shoulder was on fire.

McCrea was on his knees now. Petersen kicked him in the gut and pushed him backwards, on top of Cullen.

Through the rain of footsteps racing away from them, McCrea chundered both deep-fried lunches all over Cullen.

12

Cullen stood in Petersen's neighbour's grotty bathroom, soaking, stinking and aching. He reeked of vomit that not even Glasgow's rain could clear. And his shoulder felt like it'd dislocated. Didn't even have to look at the bruise.

He dabbed at his collar with the soaked grey towel, the white cotton stained with yellow stomach acid and chunks of second-hand chips. And the *smell.* 'Where's the nearest clothes shop?'

McCrea scowled at him. 'No idea.'

'It's your spew I'm covered in, you stupid bastard!'

'How many times can I apologise?'

'Once would be fine.'

'Look, I'm sorry.'

'You let him go, Damian.'

'So did you.'

Cullen chucked the towel into the avocado bathtub on top of the other towel. '*We* let him go. Fine. I'll clear it with Methven and own it.' He still caught that rancid stench.

'Here.' McCrea held out Cullen's baton. 'Just lying on the street. Boy must've chucked it after he battered you with it.'

Cullen put his baton into the holder at his back and stepped out into the hallway. Through in the kitchen, DC Angela Caldwell was pouring tea for the neighbour, a skinny old man who was almost as tall as she was. A shake of the head from her showed she wasn't getting much useful for Cullen, so he left the flat and went out into the stairwell to check on the paramedics' progress.

In Petersen's hallway, Bain lay on a stretcher on the floor, still just in the nappy, singing: 'Have I told you lately that I love you?' His eyes were glazed over. 'Both of you.' They covered his belly with a sheet and the female paramedic nodded at Cullen. 'We're taking him to Gartnaval. Ask for Dr McGovern, she's the specialist for... this kind of thing.'

'What kind of thing is that?'

'Date rape.'

'He's been roofied?'

'No.' She scowled. 'MDMA.'

'So, ecstasy?'

'Right, with a side order of sildenafil.'

'Eh?'

'Vitamin V.' She rolled her eyes at his continuing ignorance. 'Viagra, you tube.' She backed out of the small flat, followed by Bain, then her colleague shuffling out and bearing most of his weight.

Cullen was merciful to not see anything under the nappy.

McCrea shook his head, but there was a trace of a grin on his lips. 'Pretty fucked up, eh?'

'Come on, let's a have a look round before the forensics guys turn up.' Cullen tapped McCrea's arm, right where Petersen had hit him with Cullen's baton, right where it'd hurt the most.

'Ah, you bastard!'

'Sorry.' Cullen went into the living room, a square box.

The blinds in the kitchen area were still all mangled from his sharp exit. A flatscreen TV was mounted above a two-bar fire. No games consoles wired in, just a Fire stick poking out of the side. Maybe one of those ones some bloke down the pub had hacked to let it access countless pirate streams.

A bottle-green sofa almost the exact colour of Cullen's beloved old Golf, long since written off after a stupid chase on the streets of this infernal city.

The room stank of stale cigarettes, with a patch of yellow

above the sofa. Either Petersen, or the previous occupant, maybe an old pensioner who smoked and drank themselves to death in front of a smaller TV.

All of which was a distraction from finding him.

A chipped laminate coffee table sat off to the side, almost butting up against the kitchen units. An overstuffed ashtray sat on top, so maybe it was Petersen who was the chain-smoker.

Wait, what was that?

Wedged between the table and the sofa was a black laptop. Not a recent model, huge, should be described as a tabletop.

Cullen snapped on some gloves as he perched on the settee to open it up. Bastard thing asked for a password. Luckily, it was old enough that it didn't have those security measures that bricked the thing if you entered too many wrong guesses.

He visualised Petersen. South African. A binman. Topless. Ripped. That dragon tattoo climbing his neck.

He tried "dragon", "DRAGON", and any number of variations, "dr4gon" in both upper and lower case. Nothing.

He tried a few variations on "Springbok" and anything South African he could think of, but nothing got him in.

McCrea peered over, frowning. 'You playing *Football Manager* or something?'

'Found anything?'

'Just lube and condoms.' McCrea held up a clear evidence bag containing some pills. 'Possible this is what he used on the gaffer.'

Cullen frowned. He typed "molly" and still didn't get in. 'Christ.'

McCrea leaned forward. 'Try "lawn tennis", all one word, lower case.'

'What?'

'Just try it.'

Cullen typed it. 'Bingo. How did you know that?'

McCrea held out a Post-It. 'Stuck to the bottom.'

Cullen checked the screen, now filled with Petersen's email. Cullen had a scan through, but it was just receipts and newsletters. He typed Marie into the search bar and found just one email from her, so their friendship was most likely based on phone calls or text messages, either SMS, iMessage or WhatsApp.

Cullen couldn't remember seeing Petersen's phone. Maybe he didn't have one, but that seemed unlikely. He looked up at McCrea. 'You ever see a phone on Petersen?'

'The gaffer warned me about you. You're a phone tart, aren't you?'

'Damian, I'm trying to track down a murderer. His phone is the best way to do that. If he's got an iPhone or a generic Android smartphone, we might be able to use this machine to find him.'

'He gave us a mobile number, right? Means he's got one.' McCrea clicked his fingers a few times then winced. 'Ah shite, I did see it. One of those Nokias. Like the old burner ones, but with a battery that lasts months between charges.'

Meaning they had no chance in finding him using this laptop. Cullen rested in on the side table and stood up, getting a fresh stab of pain in his shoulder. He eased his own phone out of his pocket and called Elvis.

He answered immediately. 'Gordon's phones and CCTV, how can I help?'

'Mate, you busy?'

Elvis gave a deep sigh. 'No, but I suspect I'm about to be.'

'Need you to trace a mobile number for me.'

'Text it through, I'll see what I can do.'

Cullen took the phone away from his ear and grabbed hold of McCrea's mobile, then tapped Petersen's number into a text. 'Got it?'

'Aye, gimme a sec.' Elvis snorted. 'Bad news is it's off right now.'

'What's the good news?'

'Last time it was on was half an hour ago. Hit the same cell towers as you just now.'

'You're tracking me?'

'Methven's been looking for you. So I had a wee search for you.'

'Paul, that's illegal.'

'Aye? And half the shite you get up to isn't?'

'Tell him I'm following Bain to Gartnaval Hospital. I'll see him there.' Cullen killed the call. 'Damian, those drugs you found. Is that the same as your serial rapist?'

McCrea nodded slowly. 'Pretty much.'

'What's missing?'

'Well, him attacking Bain and killing Paul Skinner... Doesn't fit.' McCrea frowned. 'You think he was going to rape him?'

'Given he'd put the nappy on, I'd think he wasn't and was probably just going to murder him.' Cullen looked around the room one last time. 'Okay, guard the place until forensics arrive, okay?'

'Want me to see what I can get off this laptop?'

'Leave it to the professionals.'

McCrea brightened, most likely at the prospect of guarding an empty flat. 'Mind if I raid the boy's freezer?'

'You can't be hungry again.'

'It's a constant struggle, mate.'

'Of course you can't.' Cullen left him to it, but each step made the reek of vomit that bit stronger.

13

'Fuck me.' Bain lay in his hospital bed, the sheet pulled up to his neck. 'Feels like someone's fucked my head with a nailgun.'

The doctor grinned at him. 'Nobody's penetrated any part of you.'

'Eh?'

'No lasting damage, but we are going to monitor your vital signs for the next twelve hours and you should be fine. As for your erection, that should diminish on its own in the next three to four hours.'

Cullen grinned at her. 'You mean he'll stop declaring his love for me?'

'Here's hoping.' She laughed. 'I need to check something. Be right back.' She stepped through the crack in the curtains into the rest of the ward.

'I'll see where Methven's got to.' Cullen followed her through and checked his phone. Nothing. 'Need me to change your nappy?'

'Fuck off.' Rustling sounds came from behind the curtains. 'If anyone hears about this, you're fuckin' dead. You hear me?'

'You're asking me to keep it out of my report?'

'Sundance, I'm begging you. Don't make me beg.'

'You need to get the doctor, the paramedics, McCrea and all

the staff at the hospital to falsify their reports too.' Cullen gave him a few seconds. 'Brian, you're a victim. Please, tell me what you remember.'

Bain was huffing and puffing behind him. What the hell was he up to in there? 'I went in, asked the boy a few questions. Next thing I know you're standing over me and the room's fuckin' spinning.'

'You remember telling me you loved me?'

'Fuck off, Sundance.'

'You did. Want to have my babies.'

'Fuck. Off. Can't believe that bastard got us.'

Cullen shook his head. 'How? Did you have a cup of tea or something?'

'Hardly.' The doctor was back, with a grimace. 'He was attacked and knocked out, then plied with ecstasy. There's a blunt force trauma to his skull. Which is one of the thickest I've ever encountered.'

'Shut up.'

'I'm serious. If it wasn't for your Cro-Magnon cranium, you'd be dead or in an induced coma. Be thankful for your thick bone.'

'Show you a thick bone, darling.'

She rolled her eyes at Cullen. 'Don't confuse the effects of the Viagra with anything else.'

Bain huffed and huffed behind Cullen. He muttered something.

Methven was in the corridor, staring into space, jangling change in his pocket. He looked up and flashed his eyebrows at Cullen. 'Well, this is a sodding disaster.'

'Sir, as much as I want to take full ownership of this, DS Bain entered the suspect's property alone, against my orders.'

'Mm.'

'The suspect overpowered DS Bain, drugged him and possibly sexually assaulted him.' That made Methven raise his wild eyebrows. 'We'll know more when the rape kit is analyzed. And that's on him. Myself and DC McCrea were forced to enter to rescue DS Bain, where we found him drugged and wearing a nappy. Petersen was too much of a match for the pair of us. If it'd been all three of us plus DC Hunter and DC Gordon, well, it would've been a different story.'

The curtain swooshed open behind him.

Methven looked over Cullen's shoulder. 'Sodding hell, Brian, put it away.'

Cullen turned back round.

Curtains open wide, Bain was buttoning up his shirt, his distended belly hanging over his trousers, which had a tell-tale bulge at the front.

Cullen shut his eyes like he could delete the image from his head. 'My god.'

'Trying to get changed in fuckin' peace. Pair of fuckin' creeps lurking around my fuckin' bedside.'

Methven left him a lingering look, then frowned. 'Why did you go in alone?'

'Boy was heading out.' Bain sat on the edge of his bed. 'Only chance for us to catch him.'

'I don't know if you've noticed, but he escaped from our clutches.'

'Right enough. Worth a go, though. Just because I got into a bit of a swedge when I tried to apprehend the suspect doesn't mean it was a stupid idea.' Bain shot Cullen a glare, whispering: 'Warning you.'

Methven wagged a finger at Cullen, then grunted. 'What I don't understand is why Petersen tried to date rape you.'

Bain's eyes bulged. 'Who said anything about rape?'

'Well, he plied you with MDMA and Viagra, didn't he?'

'After knocking me out.' Bain shook his head. 'But he put a nappy on us. Hard to stick his boabie up my arse if I've got a fuckin' nappy on!'

'The doctor's performed a rape kit on him, we'll know the results soon enough.'

Bain's skin had gone even paler.

'He wanted to kill him.' Cullen winced. 'This is the same MO as the serial rapist McCrea's been investigating. Drugged, nappies, dumped in a bin. Bain was lucky to get out of there alive.'

Bain swallowed hard. 'Jesus fuckin' Christ.'

Methven frowned like he was trying to process it all. 'Given that Skinner and Bain weren't raped, you're saying it looks like Petersen's escalated to murder?'

'The only reason I was targeted is I was fuckin' closing in on the arsehole.'

But Cullen didn't quite buy it. 'Look, I agree that Petersen's likely our guy for those rapes, but what I don't get is why escalate to murder? Rape is all about power, domination and control. What's the benefit of adding murder to that? Why would Petersen leave Iain Farrelly's home with Paul Skinner if he intended to kill him? There's got to be some sexual motivation in there somewhere.'

'I'll fuckin' sexually motivate you.' Bain tucked his shirt back in and scowled at McGovern. 'Doc, can I get out of here?'

She smiled at Cullen. 'Trouble is, I need someone to supervise him.'

'Babysit him, more like.'

'You said it.'

Cullen spotted McCrea lumbering towards them, biting into a Mars bar like it was a grenade pin. 'I've got the perfect candidate.' He set off to meet him, catching him halfway to the stairwell door. 'What are you doing here?'

'Got relieved back at the flat.' McCrea gave him a strange wink. 'Some boy with mad lamb-chop sidies turned up asking about the laptop.'

Elvis. As far as Cullen knew, he was IT forensics trained. 'You know if he found anything?'

'No idea, man. How's the gaffer?'

'Go and have a look.' Cullen let him go, but got out his mobile and called Elvis.

'I'm looking, I'm looking.'

'And are you finding anything?'

'This isn't exactly in my wheelhouse, Scott.'

'In your what?'

'You know what I mean.'

'Okay, so can you please take it to Charlie Kidd back in Leith Walk.'

'Right, so you don't want to hear what I've just found?'

'Stop pissing about! I'm not in the mood!'

'Cool your jets. An email from KLM just landed on Petersen's laptop, confirming a flight from Glasgow to Windhoek. One-way, departing in ninety minutes.'

Cullen's turn to frown. 'Where the hell is Windhoek?'

'Capital of Namibia.' Methven stood there, nostrils flaring. 'Why?'

'Petersen might be flying there.'

Methven set off at a furious pace. 'Well, we need to get to the sodding airport!'

14

Cullen sprinted through the departure lounge, pressing his mobile hard against his ear. 'Have you got hold of him yet?'

'Negative.'

Cullen picked up his pace, tearing across the carpet floor behind Methven. The board showed Gate 10 for the KLM flight to Amsterdam Schiphol.

Closed.

He sprinted past Gate 8, then bumped through the queue at Gate 9, winding out into the walkway.

'Police! Coming through!'

Gate 10 looked ominously empty, just the ground staff speaking into handsets, yawning into fists.

Methven was at the left-hand desk, shouting at the attendant.

Cullen stopped next to the other desk, fumbling his warrant card onto the floor. He needed to try the calm and rational approach and maybe get some results. 'I need... to get on board that plane... Now. Please.'

'Sir, I'm afraid it's too late. The flight's airborne.'

Cullen looked out of the window at the plane leaving the runway. At Petersen escaping justice. He sucked in breath. 'There's a man wanted for murder on board.'

She frowned at a screen. 'I'm sorry, sir, but it's wasn't possible.'

'But the Chief Constable of Police Scotland phoned ahead and—'

'Sir, this isn't my fault, so I request you lower your voice.'

'I'm not shouting!' Cullen pocketed his warrant card. Sweat drenched his back. His legs were on fire now, not just his shoulder.

She led him a few steps away from the desk. 'Sir, this is an operational matter between your people, flight control and the bosses in Amsterdam. As much as I want to help, I just can't. I tried. Believe me. I'm really sorry.' She used a smile that might disarm a ten-pint drunk too shit-faced to get aboard a flight to Prague, but too drunk to realise it.

Cullen tried his best ten-pint drunk smile, the one that'd always get him past bouncers into a nightclub. 'Can you radio the captain or the head air steward and confirm that he is actually onboard?'

'Fine.' She walked back to her desk and it looked like she was packing things away rather than checking.

Methven joined Cullen, his face like ice and thunder. 'Well?'

'He's gone, sir.'

'I can't believe we've sodding lost him.'

'Happened to Craig Hunter a couple of years ago.'

Methven just grunted.

The attendant called over: 'Sir, the flight's via Amsterdam. Looks like Mr Petersen has a three-hour layoff before our flight to Windhoek, so you might luck out there.'

Methven seemed to collapse in on himself. 'A three-*week* layover wouldn't be enough. We'd need to get a European Arrest Warrant fast-tracked and it takes a long time. Meanwhile Petersen could be anywhere.'

Cullen nodded. 'Craig tried that too.'

'Ah yes, your ex-partner was involved.'

'You mean Chantal?'

'Not in a police sense.' Methven narrowed his eyes. 'I meant DI McNeill.'

'Right.' Cullen gritted his teeth, but didn't want to give

Methven any satisfaction. 'If I remember, it was going to take forever to come. Like you say, three weeks wouldn't do it.'

'Meanwhile, Petersen's on his way to sodding Namibia.' Methven scowled. 'Namibia doesn't have an extradition treaty with the UK. Until Mr Petersen decides to hop over the border to South Africa, we're sodding snookered.'

Cullen stared hard at him, fury burning everywhere, but especially in his shoulder. Felt like Petersen had reopened an old wound. 'I'm not giving up.' He walked back over to the desk. 'You got anything?'

'Thanks, Mags.' The attendant had the phone handset to her ear, avoiding looking at Cullen. 'I'll wait.'

Her screen showed the flight manifest, with Richard Petersen in seat 17A.

Cullen waved a hand in front of her face. 'Is he onboard?'

She rolled her eyes at him and pulled the handset away from her mouth. 'Do you want me to help or not?'

Cullen held up his hands. 'Sorry.'

'His passport and boarding pass were scanned, but we don't know if he actually got on the plane.' She put the handset back to her head then looked away from him. 'What's that, Mags?' She frowned, then turned back to Cullen. 'His seat's empty.'

Hope surged deep in Cullen's gut. 'He's not onboard?'

'Steady. They're just checking the bathrooms.'

The hope now burned in Cullen's chest. If Petersen wasn't onboard, where would he go?

Cullen scanned the departure lounge again. This area was far from the shops and the food places. The boarding flight in the next gate was in the last gasps, a stroppy teenager arguing the toss with the desk attendant. Another two live flights in the adjacent five gates, one with a series of queues, the other just full of anxious travellers glancing at the ground staff, waiting for the announcement and the ensuing scuffle.

No sign of Petersen in either.

So again, where would he go? His ticket let him get through security but it would only let him board that Amsterdam flight and that was with ID, so no chance he could swap tickets with someone else. To change it, he'd need to get back to the front desk the other side of security, and any payments would likely show up on the laptop Elvis was playing with.

But how could he know they were on to him?

Was he even here? Had the ticket been an elaborate ruse, knowing they'd find his ticket receipt on his laptop or a transaction on his current account?

One crumb of comfort was it didn't seem to fit the little Cullen had seen of Petersen.

Methven joined him. 'You're sure this isn't a red herring? It's mighty convenient that we found his boarding pass in an email.'

'I have thought that.' But Cullen couldn't face the alternative, that Petersen had hoodwinked them. Then again, it'd mean he was still on British soil and they actually had a hope in hell of catching him.

Cullen got the attendant's attention. 'Did you scan his boarding pass?'

She clicked at the keyboard. 'We did.'

'And he definitely got onboard?'

'I'd need to check CCTV.' The attendant tapped the screen. 'He's a regular flyer. He paid for this flight with points.'

Cullen pointed at the door, a gangway connecting to the plane. 'Is there anywhere else he could've gone that way?'

'Just the plane. All the doors are alarmed.'

'Did you make a call for Mr Petersen at any point?'

She nodded. 'Asked him to make himself known before boarding.'

'That's it, then.' Cullen stared at Methven. 'They spooked him. He knew we were on to him.'

Normally Cullen would rage at such utter stupidity, but this... This could be their saviour.

'So where the sodding hell is he?'

Cullen took in the area again. Further down the hall was a dead end. All the doors looked locked and alarmed. They'd come through the only entrance, maybe not checking very thoroughly, but he still couldn't see Petersen in the crowd. Meaning a good chance he was still here. 'The toilet. Stay here!'

He shot off across the walkway, muscling through a long queue of walking travellers. 'Police! Coming through!'

The toilets forked left for gents, right for ladies, straight ahead for the accessible bathroom. He tried that first, but it was empty. So he entered the gents, but slowly and carefully. A long row of sinks, an elderly man splashing water over his face at the first one, looking round at Cullen through bleary eyes.

Up ahead were urinals, sectioned off for speed and convenience, but no sign of Petersen. To the left was a long stretch of doors. Twenty, maybe thirty, on both sides. It figured; most travellers wouldn't want to splash their carry-on luggage or risk leaving it unattended anywhere.

He snapped out his baton and started opening the doors. The first couple on the right swung wide, same story on the left. The third was locked. Cullen listened.

'There's somebody there.' An English accent, whispering hard.

'Alex, just stick it in again. I won't see you for *months*.'

A couple having illicit bathroom sex before separation. Illegal, sure, but not exactly Cullen's highest priority right now.

'Rich Petersen! I know you're in here!'

The next one swung open, revealing an old man naked except for his underpants. 'For crying out loud!' He slammed the door shut and the lock rattled.

The door behind Cullen thunked open. Someone wrapped his arms tight round Cullen's throat. 'You're all mine!' Petersen, pulling Cullen back through the door. It clicked shut and the lock slid.

Cullen tried to elbow him, but he couldn't make contact.

Petersen squeezed his arm and Cullen dropped his baton.

'There are thirty cops here looking for you.'

'Fucking bullshit.'

'We know about the rapes. We know about Paul Skinner. It's over.'

Petersen tightened his grip around Cullen's throat. 'Shut your fucking mouth.' He grabbed Cullen's hair and knocked his head against the stall door.

Cullen went down like a sack of tatties. Felt like his jaw had popped out.

A boot hit his stomach and pain flared all up his body. 'You think you can take me down, eh?' Another boot, but Cullen caught it before it did too much more damage.

Not that he could do anything with it. Cullen tried to trip him up but Petersen stayed upright. Again, same result. No matter how many times he tried.

'You fucking bastard!' Petersen started punching now, hard and fast, the blows switching between crunching his ribs and his shoulder blades.

Cullen tried to block him, but they just peppered his arms like gunfire. He searched around for anything he could use as a weapon. His baton was behind the toilet, wedged in the corner.

There.

A white toilet brush, resting in a holder.

Cullen reached out for it amid a series of punishing punches to his shoulder. Felt like his arm was separating from his body. He grabbed the brush handle and pulled it out, flicking a spray of foetid water up into Petersen's eyes.

'Ah, you fucker!' Petersen covered his face with his hands, digging into his eye sockets. 'You've fucking blinded me!'

Cullen used Petersen's confusion to poke the brush into his groin, making him squeal. He grabbed his ankle from the front and tugged it.

Petersen fell backwards, cracking his head off the toilet seat.

Cullen pushed himself up to a kneel and grabbed his baton from the floor. He wedged it against Petersen' throat. 'Rich Petersen, I'm arresting you for the murder of—'

'I want a fucking lawyer!'

15

C ullen knew he shouldn't be here, given the state of him, but he needed to send Petersen down. He took the seat next to McCrea in the interview room, sipping sugary tea. He tried to roll his shoulder again and the injection's blissful numbness made him forget all about the searing pain. Another blast of it made him remember. He tried to hide his gasp with another sip of tea.

'I said, no comment.' Rich Petersen sat opposite, stinking of rubbish.

Almost made Cullen gag. He had to get up and walk around the room, otherwise he was going to lose another meal. 'Mr Petersen, let's go through this slowly. You'd drugged and trussed up my colleague in your bedroom. Detective Sergeant Brian Bain. When I burst into your flat, you fled the scene. That sound about right?'

His lawyer looked up from his silvery tablet. An elf-like beanpole in a black pinstripe who'd grown through his hair, leaving a silvery ring around his ears. 'My client is maintaining his right to silence. I believe you have to respect that, mm?'

'His right isn't transferrable. I'm going to ask as many questions as I want.' Cullen stared at Petersen, waiting for him to look up. 'Were you going to do what you did to Paul Skinner?'

'You not listening, eh? I said no comment.'

'I found my colleague trussed up in a nappy in your apartment, out of his head on the ecstasy you'd given him. Were you going to rape him? Were you going to kill him?'

'No comment.'

The lawyer had trained him well.

'Funny thing is, DC McCrea here has been investigating a few similar crimes. Men and women date raped and put in nappies, then left in bins.'

'Nappies. That's a fucking good one.'

'You were going to kill him, weren't you?'

Petersen hammered the table. 'Fuck off!'

Getting somewhere now.

'So what were you planning on doing to him?'

'No comment!'

'Because it feels a lot like it's the same person, and maybe they're escalating. Usually it starts with fire-starting. Something low level, but destructive, maybe targeted at someone who lives nearby, either to enact revenge for some perceived slight, to show off or just for kicks. But soon you've set fire to a house or a garage, and there's no reason for it now. And it doesn't stop there, does it? Because you've got away with the fires, soon it progresses to rape. Because you want to. Because you feel you deserve to have it. Then when you get away with that a few times, you realise you've got away with fires and rapes, so why not just kill them? Makes sense, doesn't it? No witnesses left to say what you did or didn't do. Whether you got consent. That sound right?'

'It wasn't me!'

A knock at the door and it cracked open. Methven's monster eyebrows were visible, along with his finger beckoning Cullen out.

'Interview paused at 15:23.' Cullen left the room and pulled the door shut behind him. 'Sir?'

Bain leaned back against the wall, silently fuming, fists clenched. He stepped forward. 'Sundance, can you keep a fuckin' lid on it, eh? Not everyone wants to hear about my... About what happened.'

'What happened to you is part of the case.' Cullen gave him a concerned look. 'The doctor happy to let you out?'

'Said I'm fine.'

'You okay?'

'Go fuck yourself, Sundance.' But Bain shut his eyes, betraying his pain.

'Whatever help you need to deal with being a victim, consider it done.'

Bain stared at him through damp eyes. 'Thanks.'

Methven joined him, clutching a machine coffee. 'Scott, I've been watching and you're not getting anything. Fast.'

'Hard to argue with that. Petersen's a psychopath, I reckon. He isn't the type to spill his guts, but he isn't the type to take the credit either, so he can brag about what he's been doing.'

'Well.' Methven pushed away from the wall and started jangling the keys in his pockets. 'There's no way Petersen is escaping this one. I'd rather he confessed, though.'

'Seen boys like him get off with anything, Col.' Bain glugged burning hot coffee like it was juice. 'Mark my fuckin' words.'

'He's a sodding murderer! He's not getting off with this!'

Dr Gibson joined them, clutching a fancy tablet. 'He's not a murderer.'

'What?'

'Colin, please don't hold this against me. My initial assessment was incorrect and it's troubled me since.'

Bain smirked. 'Darling, you've got a lot of explaining to do here.'

She ran a hand through her hair, fanning it out wide. 'I believe that, while the strangulation was peri-mortem, it wasn't the cause of death.'

'Eh?' Bain frowned at Cullen, then back at Methven. 'What killed him then?'

'Judging by the presence of what we term a totally occlusive thrombotic mass, the actual cause of death was acute myocardial ischemia.' She paused. 'A heart attack.'

'You're serious?'

She nodded. 'I reached out to James Deeley through in Edinburgh and, while he has only seen a series of snapshots and video files, James does follow my logic and agrees in principle.'

Cullen sucked breath through his teeth. Skinner died of a heart attack. 'So what the hell did happen?'

'I want you to find out.' Methven clapped his shoulder. 'Run this past Petersen. Five minutes, then we'll take a break and regroup. Okay?' He slipped off back towards the observation suite.

Cullen was losing a handle on the case. The streak-of-piss lawyer could poke holes in anything they'd done. Bain or McCrea, one or both of them would've screwed something up big time, and he'd not find out until much later.

He sloped back into the interview room and started the recorder again. 'Interview recommenced at 15:29.' He took his seat and waited till Petersen looked up at him. 'So. Mr Petersen, I want to apologise.'

He looked up with a deep frown.

'I seem to have misjudged you. I see it now, clear as day. You're a lover, not a fighter. I bet you never killed anyone. I bet Paul's death was an accident. If that's what happened, then tell me the truth about it and don't let everyone else think you're a murderer when you're not. Work with me here.'

Petersen stared at his lawyer for a few seconds, then at Cullen. 'No comment.'

'Sure about that?' Cullen left him a few seconds. 'Because, as it stands, you're going to be charged with a number of rapes. Five, is it, Damian?'

McCrea cleared his throat. 'Five, plus dumping this body. And he assaulted DS Bain, drugged him and... Well. I'd say five rapes, but it could've been six or seven.'

'And we're also going to charge you with Paul Skinner's murder as well as his rape.'

'You got scared, didn't you? I mean, rape is one thing but what do you do with a dead body. You were just having a laugh, not trying to kill anyone...'

Petersen stared at the desk. He slammed his fist into the table. Looked like it hurt, too. 'It wasn't me! He died of a heart attack!'

And there it was. Oldest trick in the book. Get the suspect to think you understand why they did what they did. Always makes a suspect more likely to confess to someone who 'gets it'.

'Turns out the cause of death for Mr Skinner wasn't the strangulation. The post mortem found that he died of a heart attack.' Cullen sat back in his chair. Heard this before. 'How about you tell me it all?'

Petersen took a few seconds to think it all through. Then he leaned over to whisper in his lawyer's ear. He got a non-committal shrug. 'I didn't rape Skinner. It was consensual.'

Cullen cracked his knuckles, loud and hard. 'There are eighty-three police officers in this building, sixty uniform and twenty-three plainclothes detectives. I'm the only one with the training, education and compassion to understand that there are always reasons. That sometimes things don't happen the way they were planned. Now, Mr Petersen, I am going to be quiet and listen. I at least want to give you that chance. Your choice whether you take it or not.'

Petersen cleared his throat. 'Right, mate, I'm telling you this because I trust you, okay? Here's what happened, eh? I was out with Marie. She's a friend of mine. Had a few cocktails, then she asked me to go back to a party at her boyfriend's. There was booze and coke and music and I don't drink, but the other two, well... So I got speaking to his bloke, yeah? Seemed like a good laugh, started dancing to Beyoncé and I said, let's get out of there. Took him back to mine. We were getting it on in my bed. I'd... I'd finished and he was still ploughing away, then he ... He just died, man.'

'Just died?'

'One minute he was pounding my arsehole, next thing I know he's a dead weight on me.'

'Why didn't you call 999?'

Petersen couldn't maintain eye contact. 'I wanted to.'

'And what stopped you? Why dump the body?'

'No comment.'

'You knew about the DNA and knew we'd tie the others to you. So you panicked and disposed of the body in a bin where you'd be collecting first thing. Then you'd get rid of the body on your rounds, but your workmate interrupted you.'

'Big fucking Jim. He ruined it all.' Petersen stared up at the ceiling. 'A fucking heart attack, man.'

'And what about DS Bain?'

'He got too close. That's it.'

'Did you rape him?'

'Of course I didn't. I've got standards.'

~

CULLEN STOOD against the back wall of the obs suite, his legs aching with the tickle of lactic acid, right up the backs of his calves and hamstrings. He hadn't run like that in ages.

Methven sat in front of him, silently fuming. He pressed the giant button on the controls and put the interview on mute.

On the screen, McCrea and Hunter were interviewing Rich Petersen, taking it all down in great detail.

It was like a tap had opened and wasn't going to stop pouring for a long time. Petersen sat still, arms folded across his chest, showing no emotion as he described in precise detail the brutality of his attacks. The only mercy was Cullen could longer hear the depravity.

Methven. 'Well, it looks like we've got enough evidence to support a conviction, I'd wager. We solved five rapes, a murder and an attack on a serving officer. Mr Petersen will be going away for a very long time. Excellent work.'

'Thanks, sir.' Cullen tried to ease his shoulder round, but pain flared. 'We were lucky.'

'Maybe, but we did well. You did well, Scott.'

'Thanks, sir.'

Methven got up and joined Cullen by the back wall, but whatever Cullen did he couldn't stop him staring right at him. 'I still need you to get your team-size review to Carolyn.'

Cullen stared up at the ceiling, the one place Methven couldn't be. 'I need two DSs. And I want to keep Bain.'

Methven laughed, shaking his head. 'You two should work together more often.'

EPILOGUE

BAIN

I lower myself in the bath and the water's fuckin' burning. Feels like my bawbag's on fire, I tell you.

Not as sore as my old fella, I'll tell you that too. That dirty South African bastard, slipping us a Viagra. What was he playing at?

Need to ignore it. Focus on the here and now.

I reach over to the edge of the bath and grab the beer. Still cold, so I take a sip and that's the fuckin' ticket. Not bad, bit too bitter for my tastes, but hoppy enough. Thinking an eight out of ten for the next podcast. Bet Elvis gives it a four, the poncy sod. Him and his fuckin' sours and *porters*. I put it back on the side and crack my bonce off the bath edge.

It hurts like buggery.

Shouldn't joke about that. That fuckin' creep was going to rape us, I know it.

And I fuckin' blame Sundance. Sending me in there on my jack. Or as near as damn it. Fuckin' Hunter should've been there too.

No, I need to take that prick down a peg or two. Time to concoct a fuckin' long firm against Sundance, something he won't see coming.

ACKNOWLEDGMENTS

Without the following, this book wouldn't exist:

Development Editing
Allan Guthrie

Procedural Analysis
James Mackay

Copy Editing
Allan Guthrie, Kitty Harrison

Proofing
John Rickards

As ever, infinite thanks to Kitty for putting up with me and all of my nonsense.

CULLEN & BAIN WILL RETURN IN

"WORLD'S END"

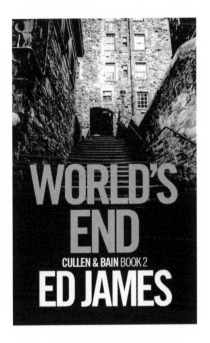

June 1st 2020

Pre-order now

If you enjoyed this book, please consider leaving a review on Amazon.

The next book in the series is on pre-order now — keep reading to the end of this book for a sneak preview. You can buy a copy at Amazon.

If you would like to be kept up to date with new releases from Ed James, please fill out a contact form.

SEE ANOTHER SIDE OF SCOTT CULLEN IN

"MISSING"

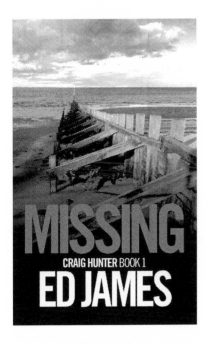

Out now!

Cullen features heavily in MISSING, a police procedural comedy thriller starring Craig Hunter, ex-soldier and ex-CID, now back in uniform.

It's out now and you can get a copy at Amazon.

WORLD'S END

EXCERPT

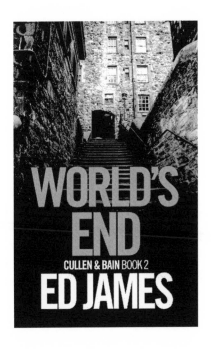

PROLOGUE

Adam stood in the freezing darkness, shivering as he stuck his key in the lock and twisted. But it didn't open. 'Bloody head office. Too cheap to pay for a proper system.' Every day, Adam saw how cheap they were, but hey, a job's a job. He tried the key again and the door opened this time, with no rhyme or reason. He took a deep breath and stepped inside the supermarket.

The lights flickered on, lifting the gloom on the breezeblock walls. But not by much. The store's backroom was a giant cube filled with empty metal cages. The deep freeze was just to the side, humming away, so he walked over to the door through to the front.

And it was absolutely boiling, like the heater had been working ten to the dozen all night. He just knew he was going to lose a couple of hours trying to get the standard-rate boiler repair guy down to Edinburgh from all the way up in Crieff. Yet more cheapness from head office.

And a stale smell hung on the air, like someone had left a packet of steak mince out all night. Or a whole cage of it. If there was one thing Adam knew, it was people leaving meat out all night. Bane of his effing life. He could picture fifty packets of mince browning and going all slimy.

'Hold the door!' Keith Ross was rushing down the street, his boots clumping off the frosty pavement, but he was a good three stone too heavy to keep that pace up for long. Not with *his* knees. He stopped, hard breath puffing in the freezing air, his distended belly hanging out of his "NO CHEMTRAILS" hoodie. In this weather, he still didn't wear a coat. Adam got a waft of dope, a tell-tale sign of yet another night on the hash bowls. At least he was wearing his official Ashworth's jacket, though the orange wasn't as bright as it should be. 'Cheers, boss. Couldn't find my key this morning.'

Adam locked the door behind him with a sigh. 'Keith, you live in Clermiston, we're in Gilmerton. That's two buses, especially at this hour. Meaning that if I insisted you went back home to collect that key, which is effing company property then I'll lose my cleaner for an hour. The hour which is the only time during the day you can do any real cleaning.'

'You seriously want me to go home?'

'No, I of course I don't. Just stop forgetting it.'

'No big deal, though, man.' Keith smiled at him. 'You're always here, bud. Or there's Have A Phil doing the bread.'

'You shouldn't call him that.' Adam waited for a nod. 'And what if Phil forgets his key and I've got the dentist?'

'The dentist at half six in the morning?' Keith's face twisted up. Cynical bastard was always trying to pick holes in stuff. But then his face brightened with some new mystery. 'You know if I quit, you'll never find anyone as cheap as me.'

Adam didn't doubt it, but then you pay peanuts, you get monkeys. 'And you'll struggle to find another job.' He gestured through the roasting backroom towards the cleaning store. 'Just get on with it, okay?'

No sign of Keith doing that. The big lump just stood there, the overhead lights lost in his thick beard. 'You check those links I sent you?'

Adam vaguely remembered some messages on his phone that morning, but he was too bleary-eyed to focus on them. The pot of coffee had cleared the worst of his hangover, but it was already shaping up to be a day where he needed to schedule a nice snooze on the toilet. 'I was busy last night, sorry.'

'Busy nudging turps, aye?' Keith stepped forward, his glassy eyes glowing in the dark store. 'Found this cracking video about coronavirus. Apparently the CIA developed it, unleashed it on some bats in China. From space.'

'How did bats get into space?'

'Don't be daft.' Keith rolled his eyes. 'They targeted the bats from an orbital platform.'

'With lasers?'

'No.' But he didn't have an answer.

Time for Adam to twist the knife. 'If the CIA did it, how does that explain it infecting people in America?'

'Collateral damage.' Keith's shrug showed that's all the consideration that gaping hole needed. 'Plus, the kind of people most at risk of catching it are the ones who can't afford to get a test and can't afford to take two weeks off work in quarantine. Thinning out the herd.'

Always an answer for everything. What Adam wouldn't give to go back in time to before YouTube and all those nut-job conspiracy theories, and before pretty much everything else. 'All so the New World Order can institute a global government, aye?'

'Sure you didn't watch it?'

'Positive.' Adam patted his arm. 'I'll just check on the young lad, see how he's getting on.' He pointed to the cleaner's store cupboard again. 'Get on with it.'

'Aye, aye. It's *boiling* in here. I'm sweating like a bastard already.'

'So turn the heating down.'

'Aye, aye.' Keith shuffled off, stuffing in his earbuds to listen to yet another conspiracy freak podcast, or an audiobook about chemtrails turning frogs gay, or whatever new nonsense he was filling his head with.

Adam walked off in the opposite direction, passing through the rubber flaps into the store itself. He hit the first aisles and triggered the banks of lights to flash on.

It was set in pitch darkness—not a good sign—so he set off, the lights flashing on as he passed. He tried not to inspect each and every aisle for how badly they needed refilling. Tuesday night wasn't nightfill, so his team of underpaid idiots would stack up during the day. The way things used to be, but it meant they'd be chasing their tails all day until the store shut and the nightfill took over.

No toilet rolls, even with their rationing at the tills. Pretty soon people would start paying for things by the sheet. Or they'd move on to pasta or tins of tomatoes.

At the far end, the bread aisle was a complete disaster. The shelves were virtually empty, just the huddled remnant of yesterday's stock that hadn't been sold off to the yellow-item vultures in the final hour of trading last night. And no sign anyone had been in this morning. Young Phil should've been here at the crack of sparrow fart to take the bread delivery and start stocking up. Should've just about been finished by now too.

He checked his phone for messages from Phil, maybe saying he was self-quarantining, but there was just the YouTube link from Keith.

Either way, looked like he was going to have to do the whole lot himself.

And it was so effing hot. Still, the sooner he started, the sooner he'd get that bacon roll and that blissful sleep on the toilet. He stomped off, the shop now all bright and glaring, then through the doors to the back storeroom.

The storeroom was piled high with boxes ready for the compactor. No sign of Young Phil.

A loud squeak came from somewhere behind him. Made him jerk around.

But it was just Keith twisting that tap he was constantly moaning about, the one Adam would have to call another Crieff-based plumber to fix.

Adam cut through the narrow corridor between the boxes, just about wide enough to wheel a cage through and opened the main door. And there they were, the bread cages, unattended and freezing in the icy blast.

Six of white, two of wholemeal, another three of rolls and wraps and all that malarkey. Two of cakes.

And still no sign of Young Phil.

Effing useless.

Adam took the first cake cage and wheeled it inside. He stopped dead.

In an alcove between some empty cages, someone had scrawled a message over the scuffed floor tiles. "Love and kisses, the Evil Scotsman".

What the effing hell?

Next to it, a body lay in an Ashworth's uniform, covered from head to toe in yellow price-reduction stickers.

Young Phil.

Was he just messing about?

Adam charged over and went to shake him. But he stopped. There was something about not waking someone who was sleepwalking, wasn't there? And... Christ. Phil wasn't breathing.

He touched Phil's cheek. Ice cold. Dead.

And Adam would have to do the effing bread on his own.

∽

You can preorder WORLD'S END now at Amazon.

If you would like to be kept up to date with new releases from Ed James, please fill out a contact form.

Made in the USA
Coppell, TX
08 June 2020

27210824R00065